HOT SHOT HOCKEY

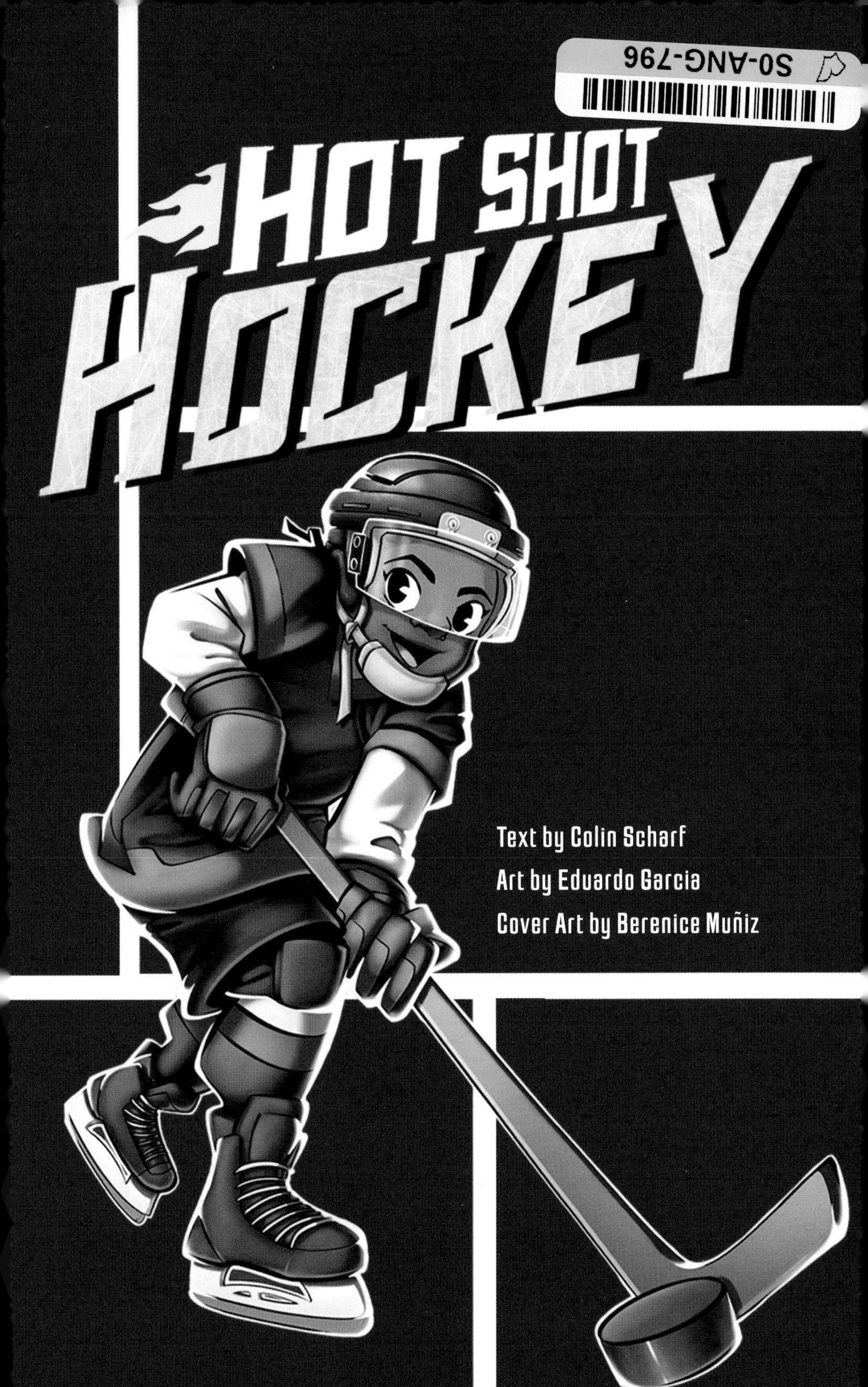

Text by Colin Scharf
Art by Eduardo Garcia
Cover Art by Berenice Muñiz

CAST OF CHARACTERS

Robyn

Grandpa
Freddie

Dad

Mom

Aggie   **Miri**   **Clara**   **Ada**

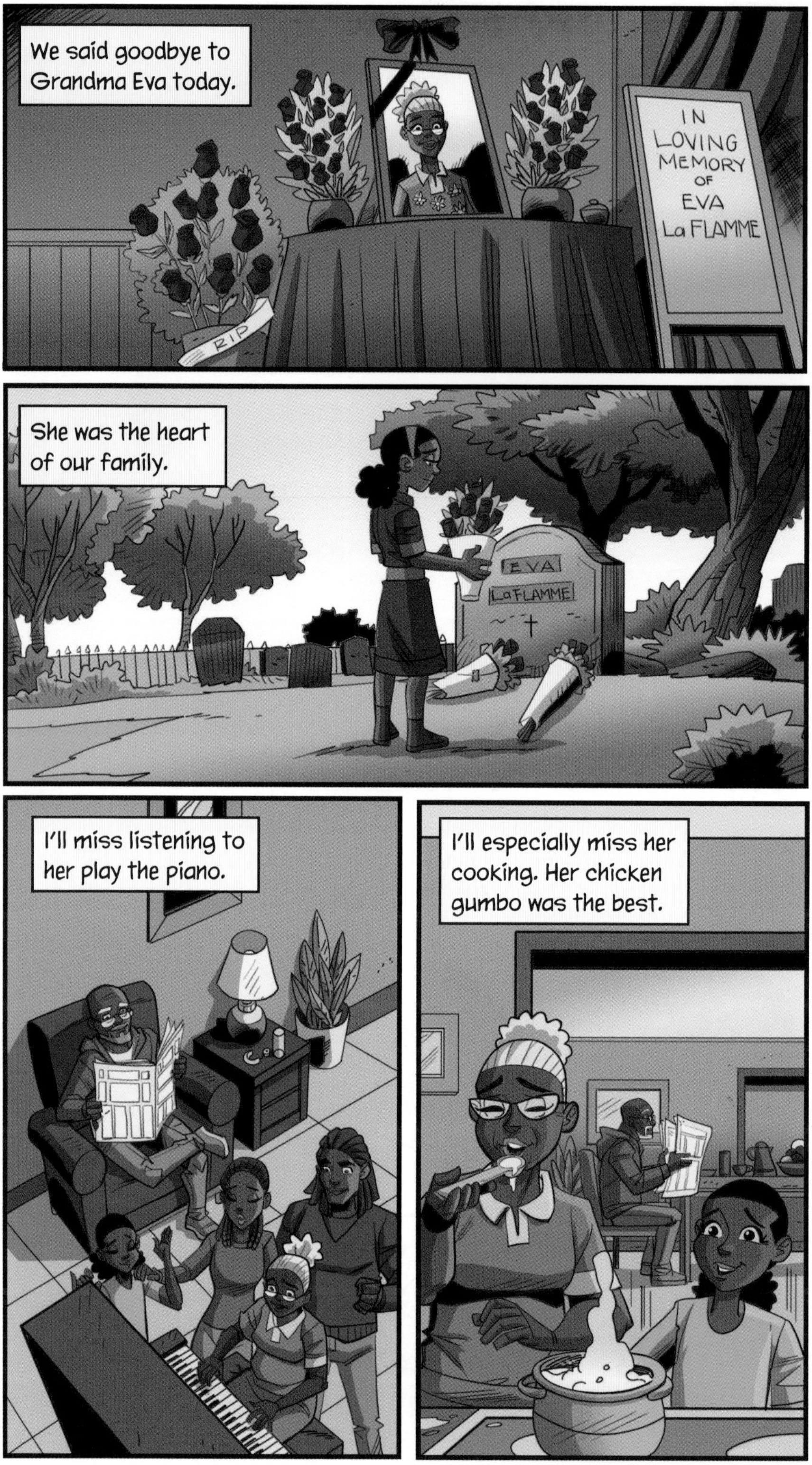
We said goodbye to Grandma Eva today.
IN LOVING MEMORY OF EVA La FLAMME
RIP
She was the heart of our family.
EVA
LaFLAMME
I'll miss listening to her play the piano.
I'll especially miss her cooking. Her chicken gumbo was the best.

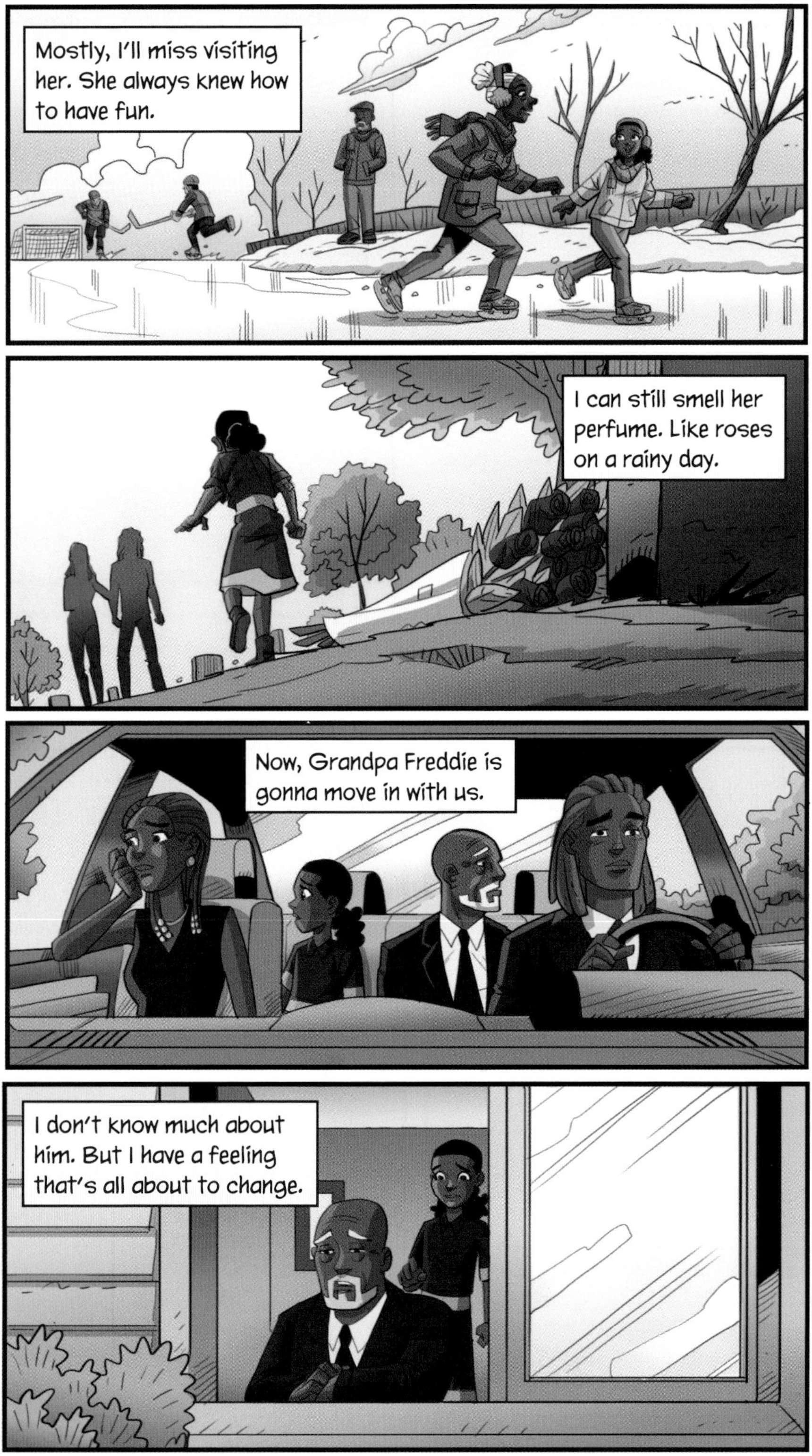
Mostly, I'll miss visiting her. She always knew how to have fun.
I can still smell her perfume. Like roses on a rainy day.
Now, Grandpa Freddie is gonna move in with us.
I don't know much about him. But I have a feeling that's all about to change.

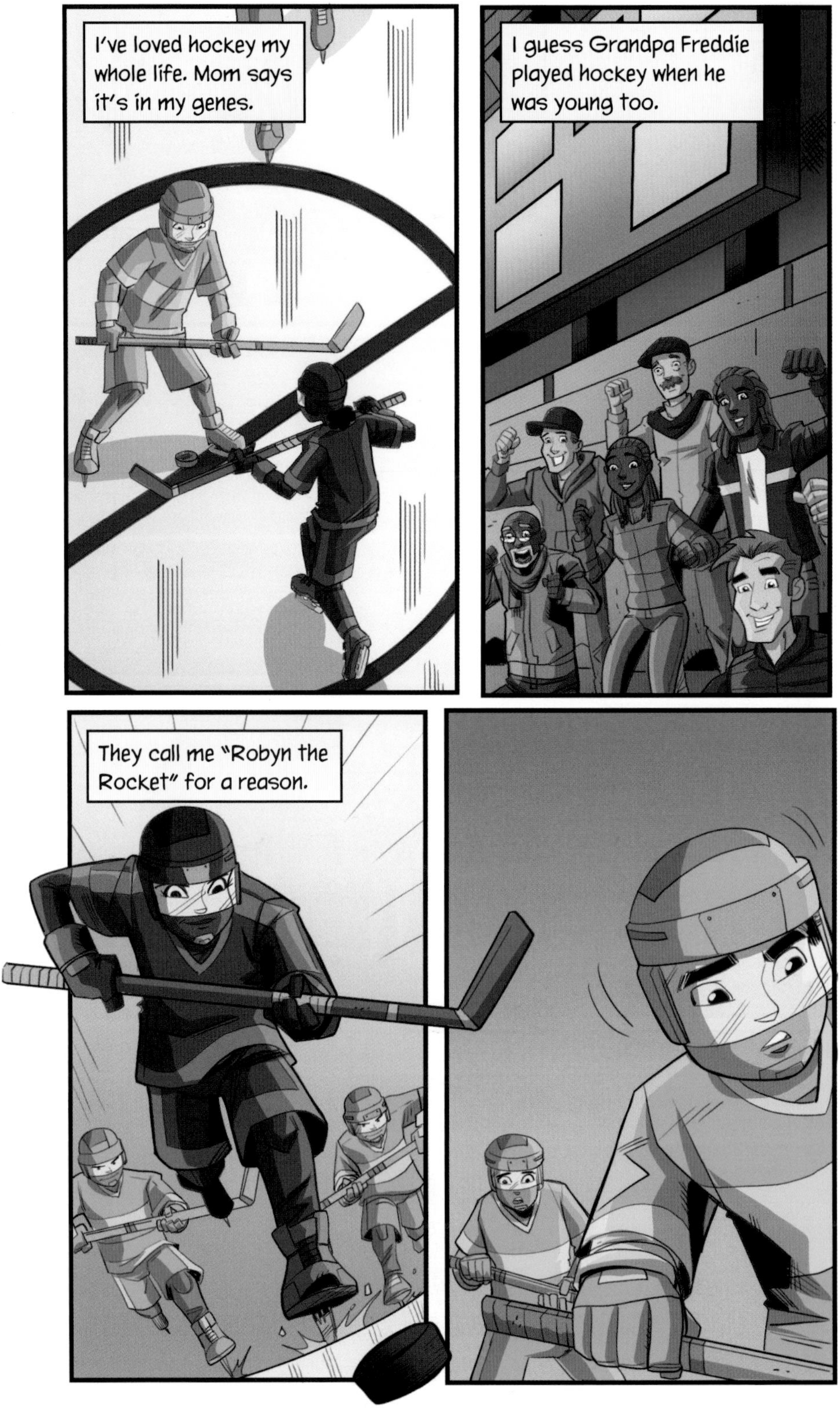
I've loved hockey my whole life. Mom says it's in my genes.
I guess Grandpa Freddie played hockey when he was young too.
They call me "Robyn the Rocket" for a reason.

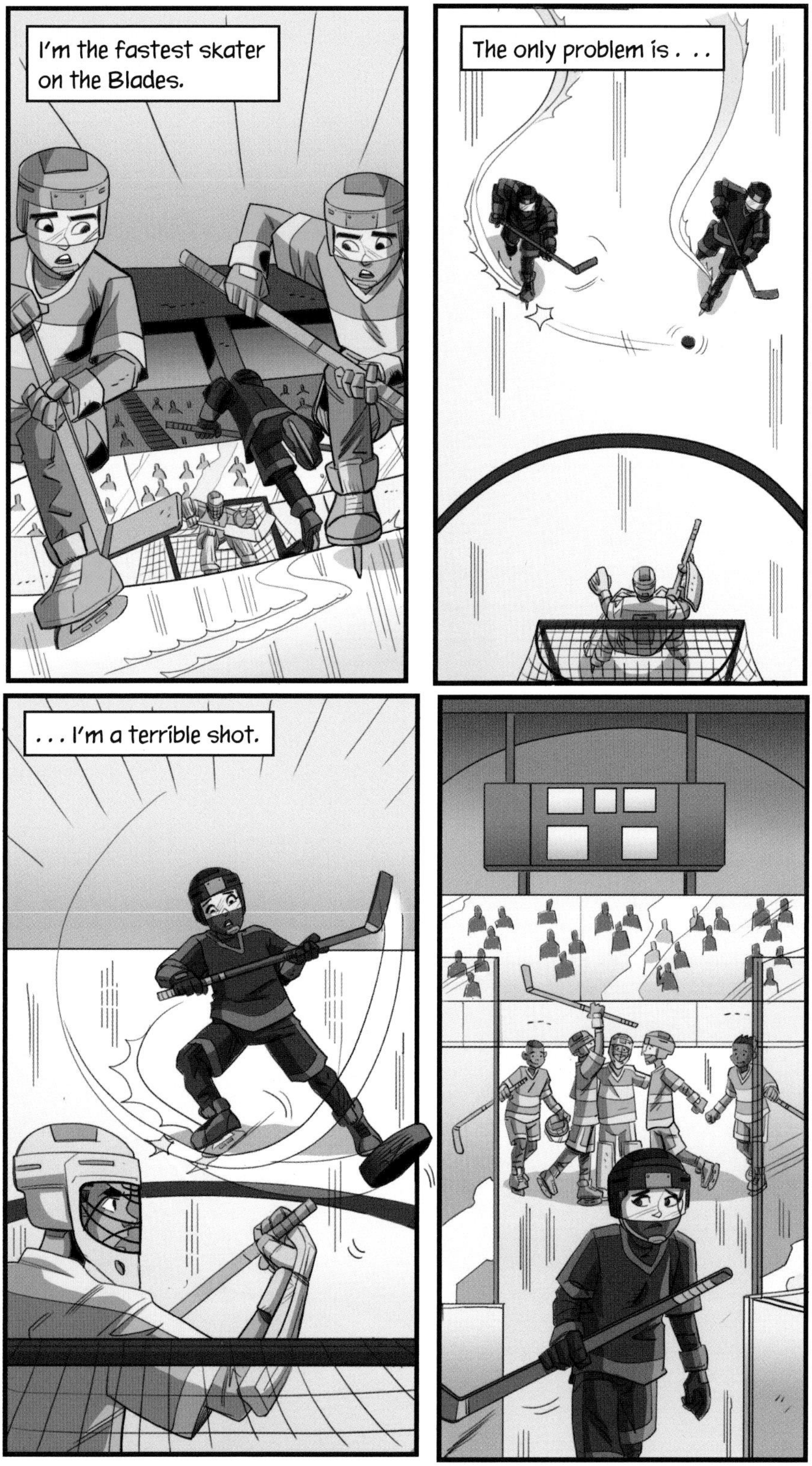
I'm the fastest skater on the Blades.
The only problem is . . .
. . . I'm a terrible shot.

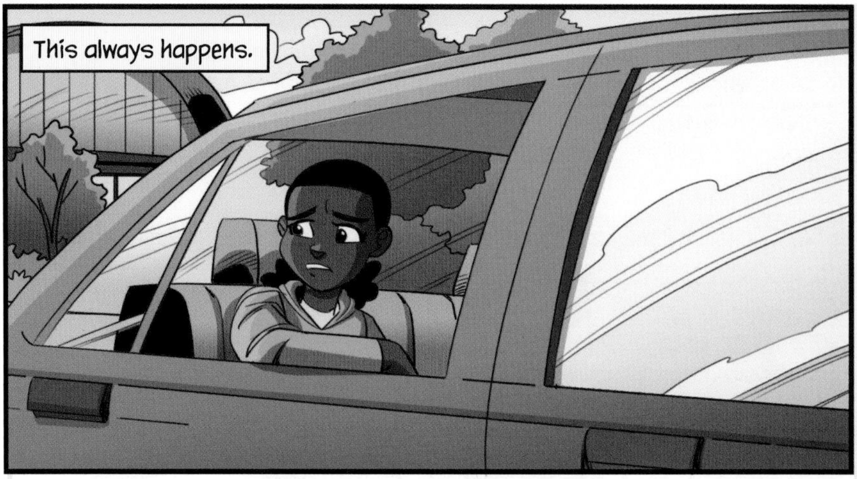
This always happens.

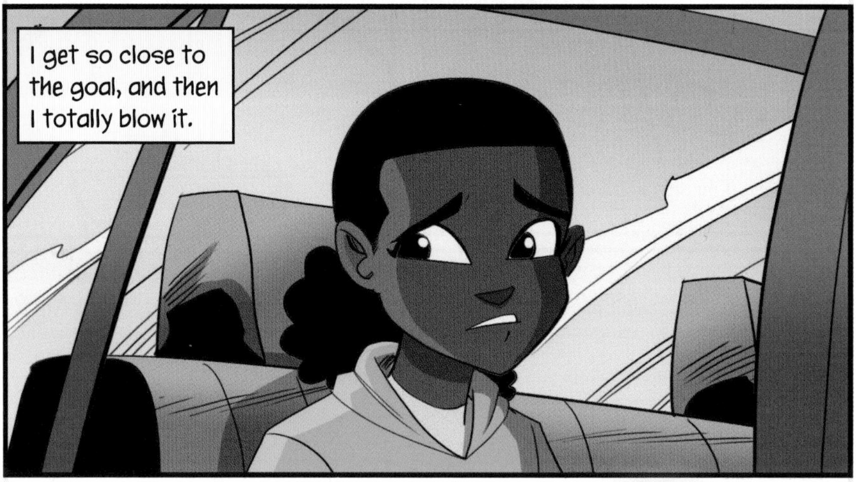
I get so close to the goal, and then I totally blow it.

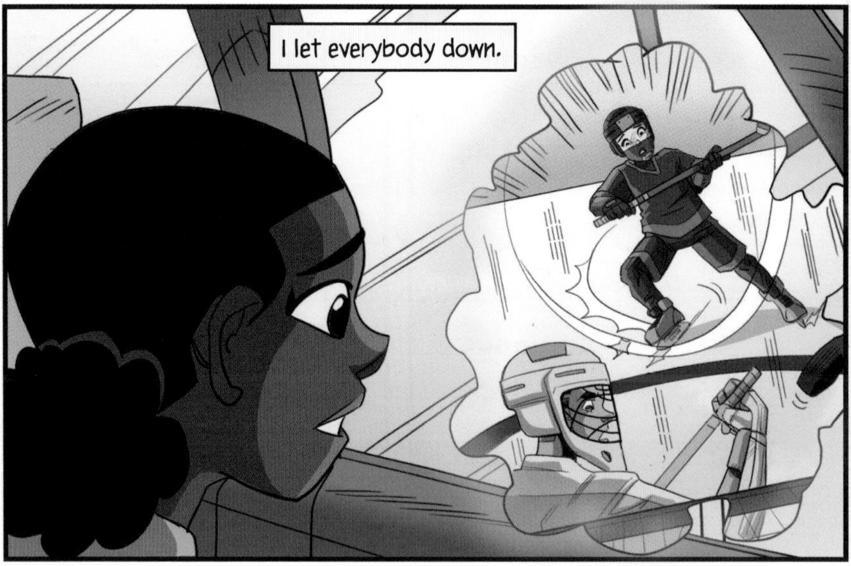
I let everybody down.

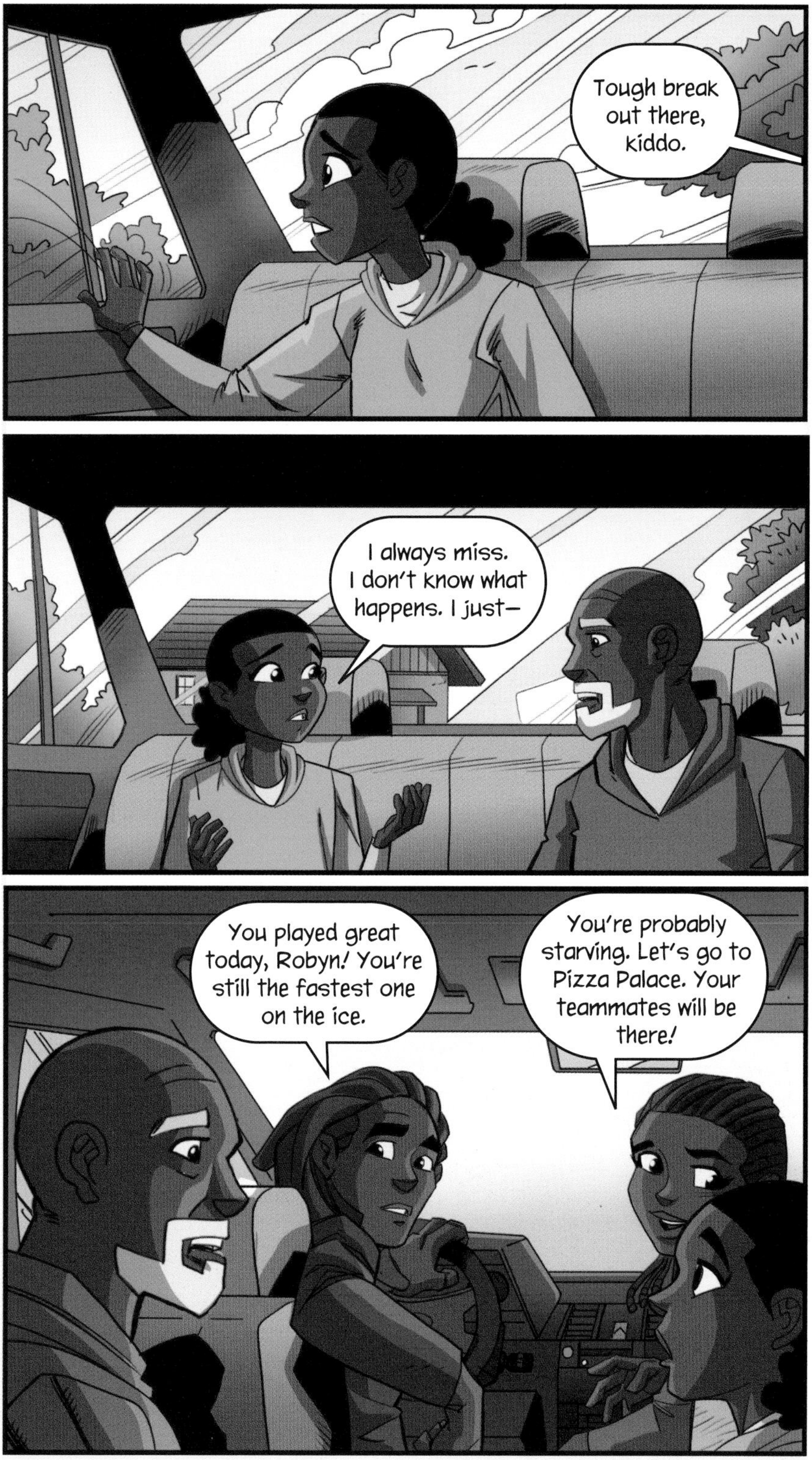
Tough break out there, kiddo.
I always miss. I don't know what happens. I just—
You played great today, Robyn! You're still the fastest one on the ice.
You're probably starving. Let's go to Pizza Palace. Your teammates will be there!

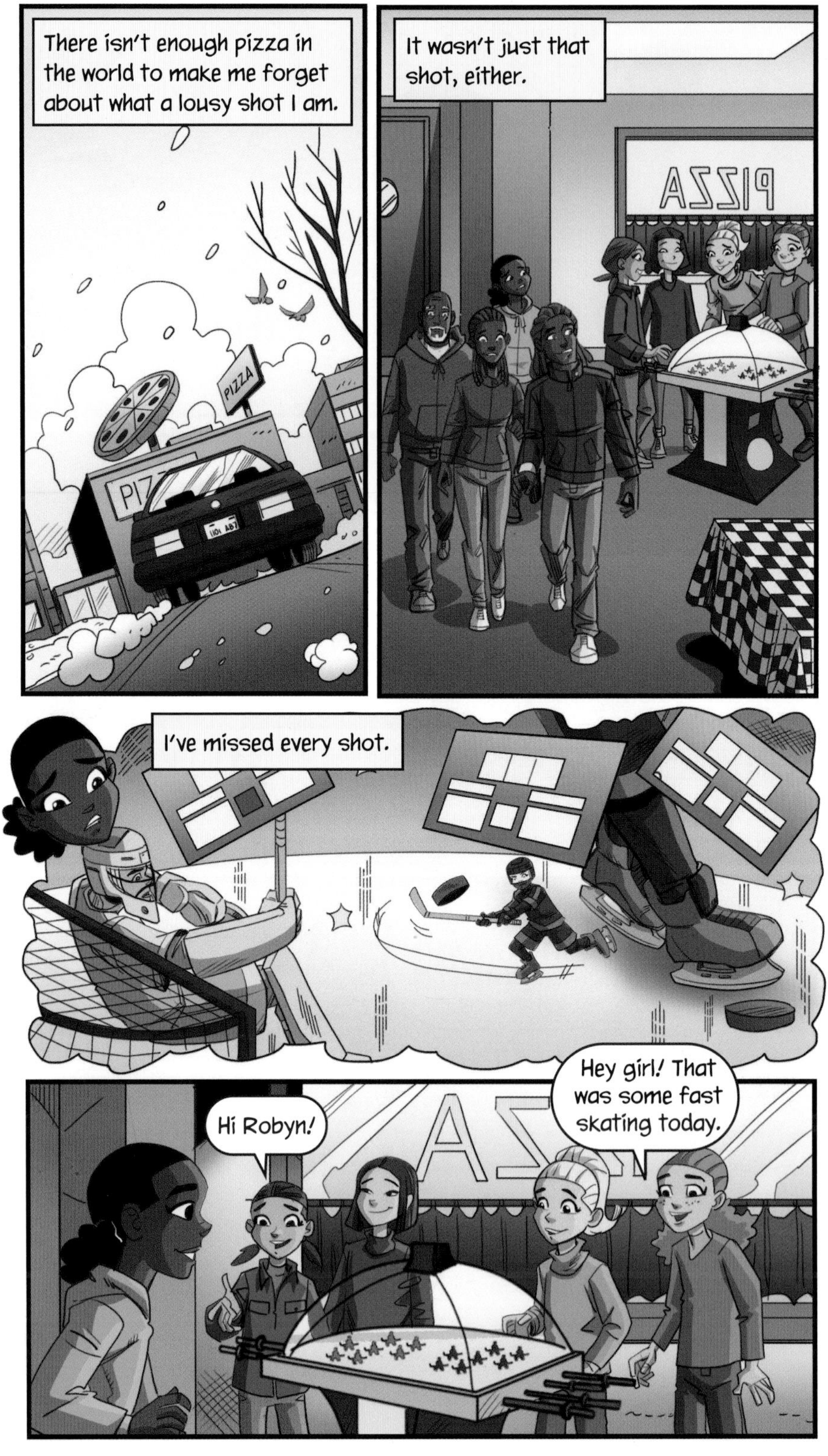
There isn't enough pizza in the world to make me forget about what a lousy shot I am.
PIZZA
It wasn't just that shot, either.
PIZZA
I've missed every shot.
Hi Robyn!
Hey girl! That was some fast skating today.

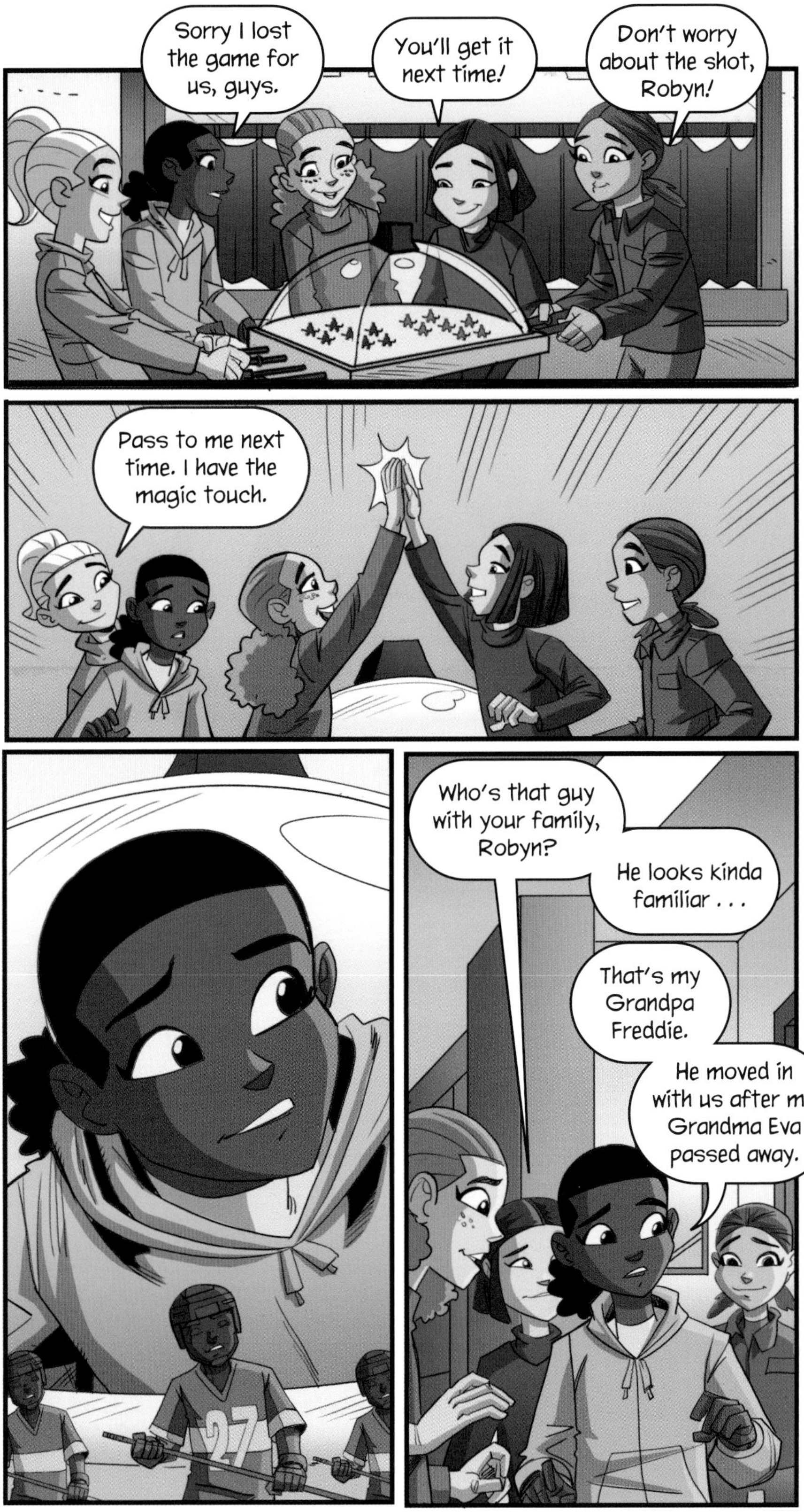
Sorry I lost the game for us, guys.
You'll get it next time!
Don't worry about the shot, Robyn!
Pass to me next time. I have the magic touch.
Who's that guy with your family, Robyn?
He looks kinda familiar . . .
That's my Grandpa Freddie.
He moved in with us after my Grandma Eva passed away.

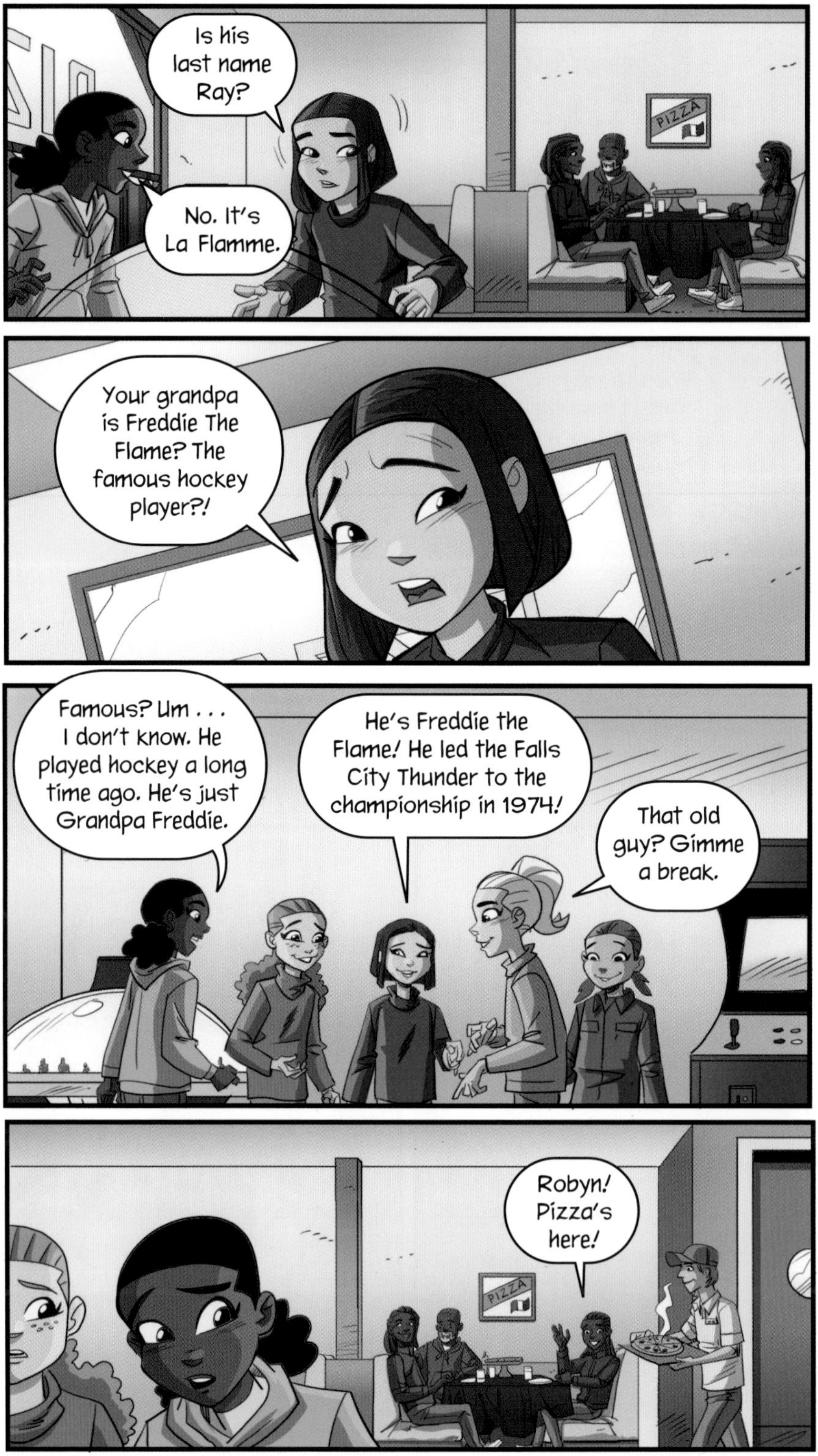

Is his last name Ray?
No. It's La Flamme.
Your grandpa is Freddie The Flame? The famous hockey player?!
Famous? Um . . . I don't know. He played hockey a long time ago. He's just Grandpa Freddie.
He's Freddie the Flame! He led the Falls City Thunder to the championship in 1974!
That old guy? Gimme a break.
PIZZA
Robyn! Pizza's here!

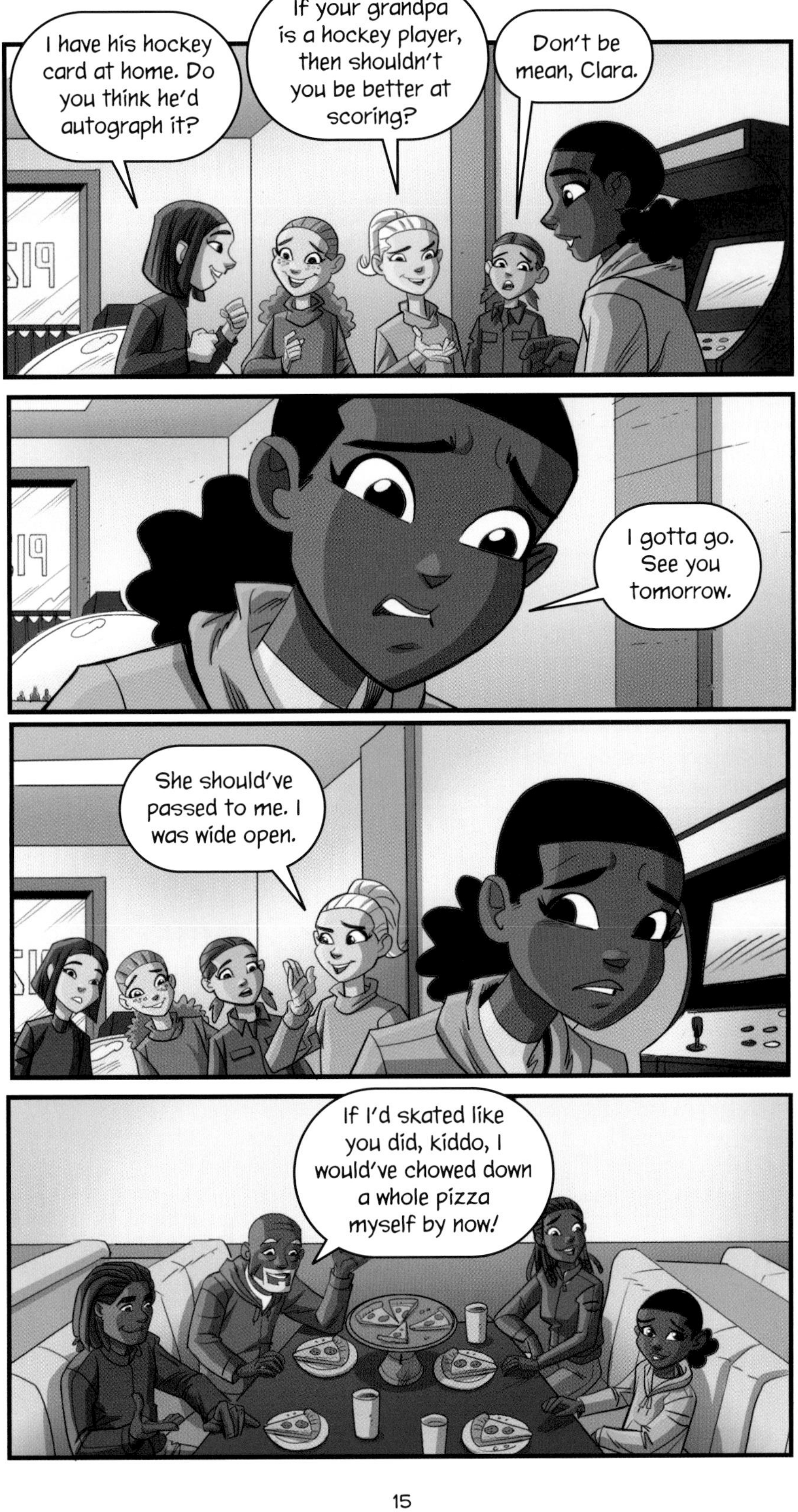
I have his hockey card at home. Do you think he'd autograph it?
If your grandpa is a hockey player, then shouldn't you be better at scoring?
Don't be mean, Clara.
I gotta go. See you tomorrow.
She should've passed to me. I was wide open.
If I'd skated like you did, kiddo, I would've chowed down a whole pizza myself by now!

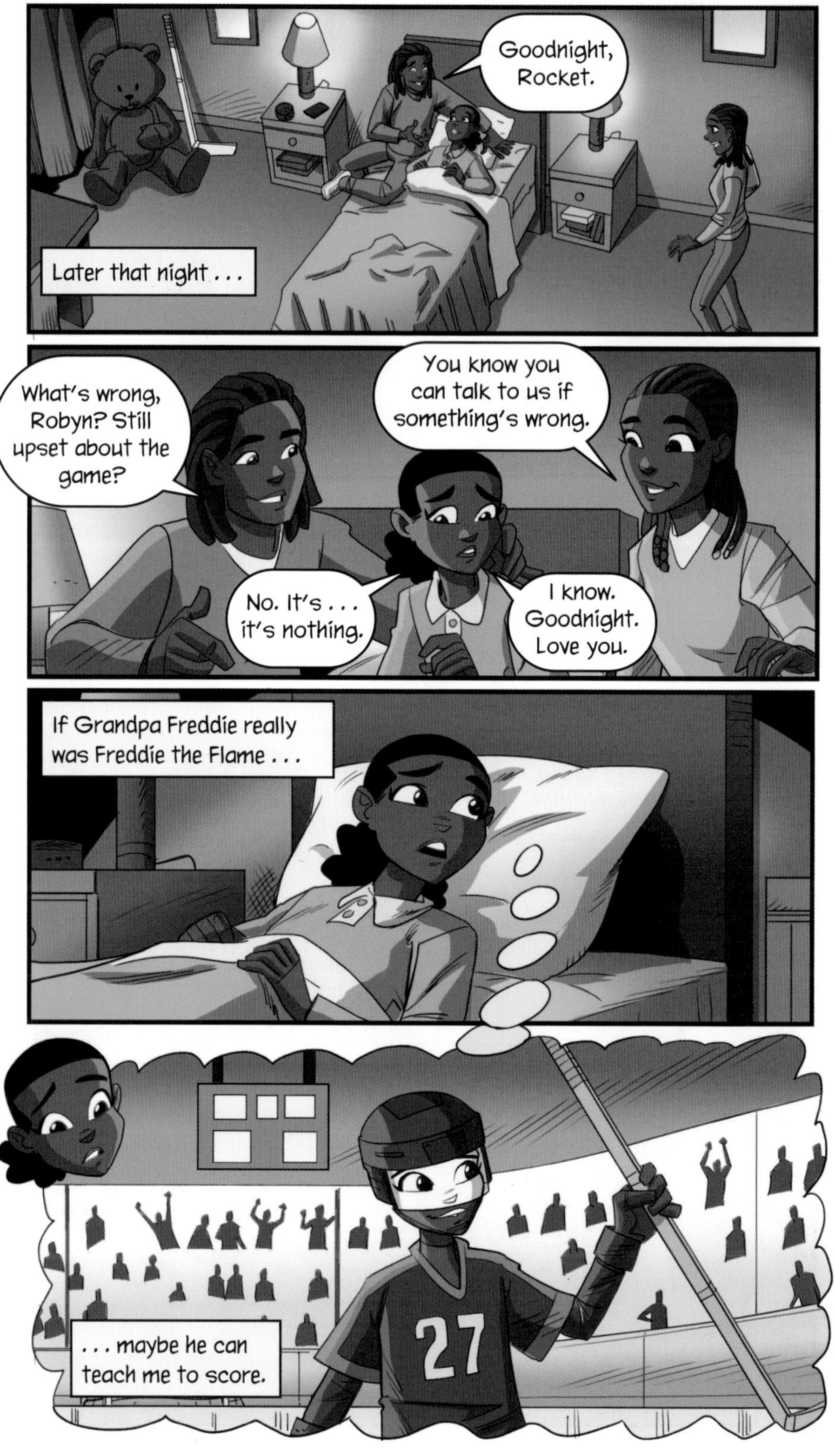
Goodnight, Rocket.
Later that night . . .
What's wrong, Robyn? Still upset about the game?
You know you can talk to us if something's wrong.
No. It's . . . it's nothing.
I know. Goodnight. Love you.
If Grandpa Freddie really was Freddie the Flame . . .
. . . maybe he can teach me to score.
27

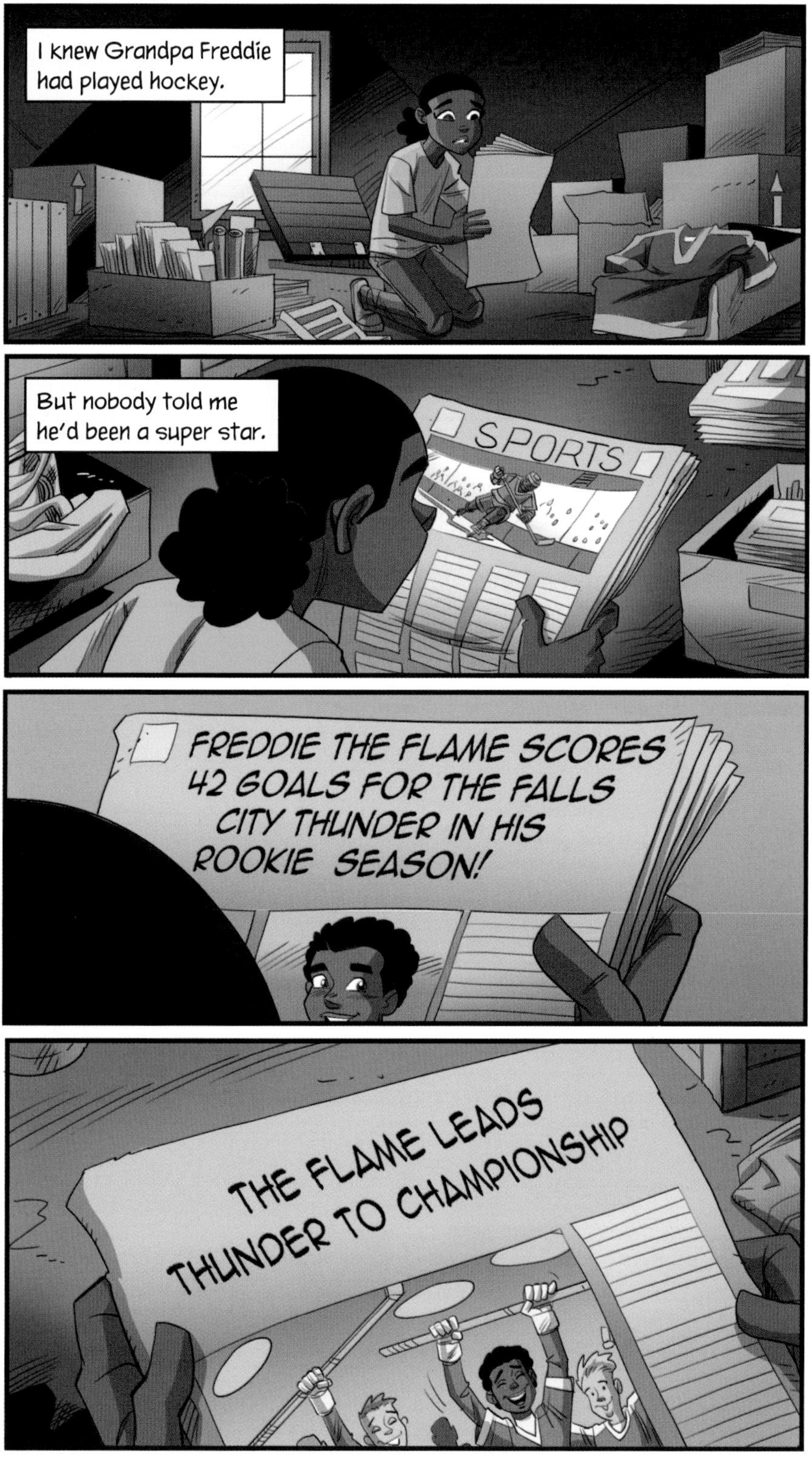
I knew Grandpa Freddie had played hockey.
But nobody told me he'd been a super star.
SPORTS
FREDDIE THE FLAME SCORES 42 GOALS FOR THE FALLS CITY THUNDER IN HIS ROOKIE SEASON!
THE FLAME LEADS THUNDER TO CHAMPIONSHIP

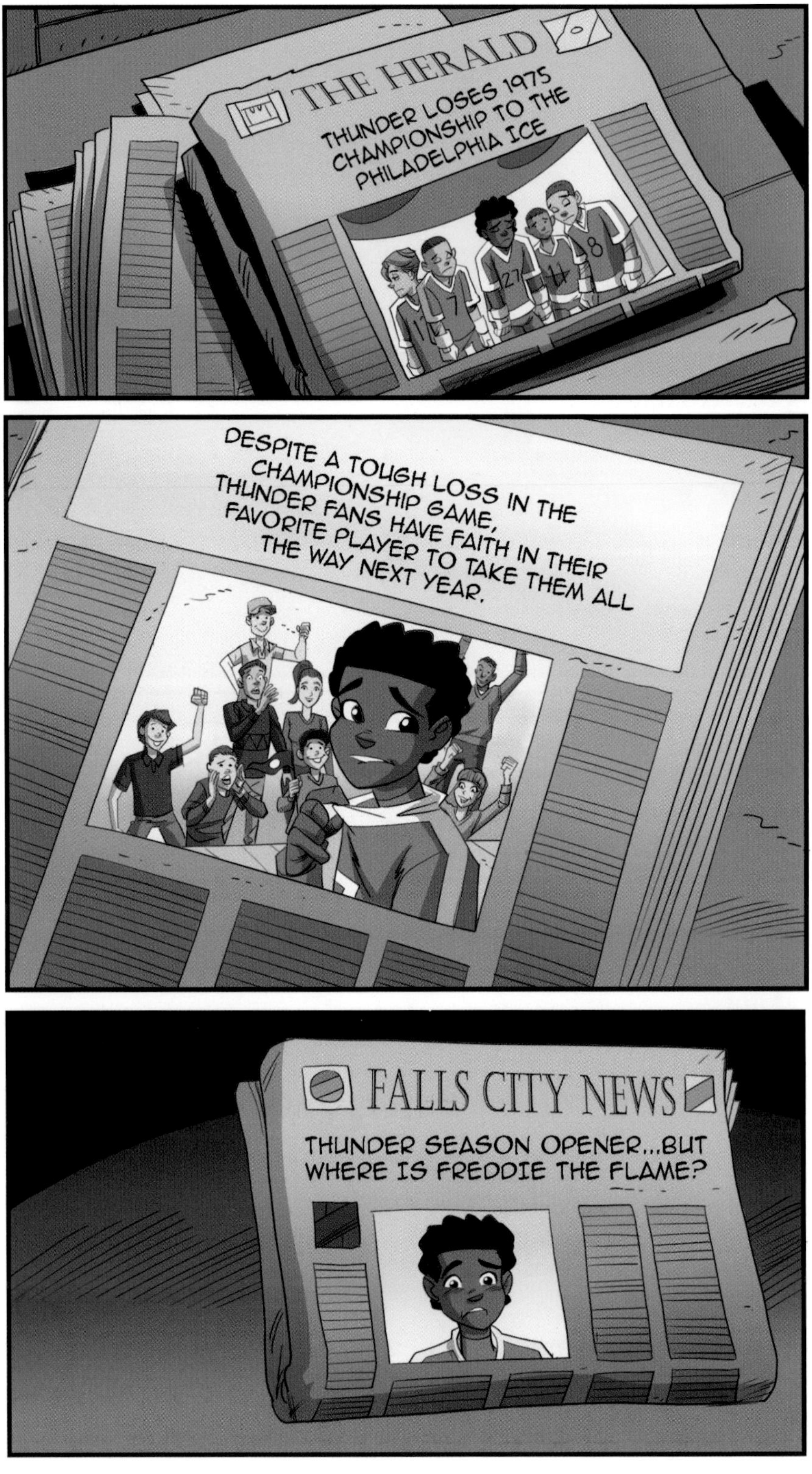
THE HERALD
THUNDER LOSES 1975 CHAMPIONSHIP TO THE PHILADELPHIA ICE
DESPITE A TOUGH LOSS IN THE CHAMPIONSHIP GAME, THUNDER FANS HAVE FAITH IN THEIR FAVORITE PLAYER TO TAKE THEM ALL THE WAY NEXT YEAR.
FALLS CITY NEWS
THUNDER SEASON OPENER...BUT WHERE IS FREDDIE THE FLAME?

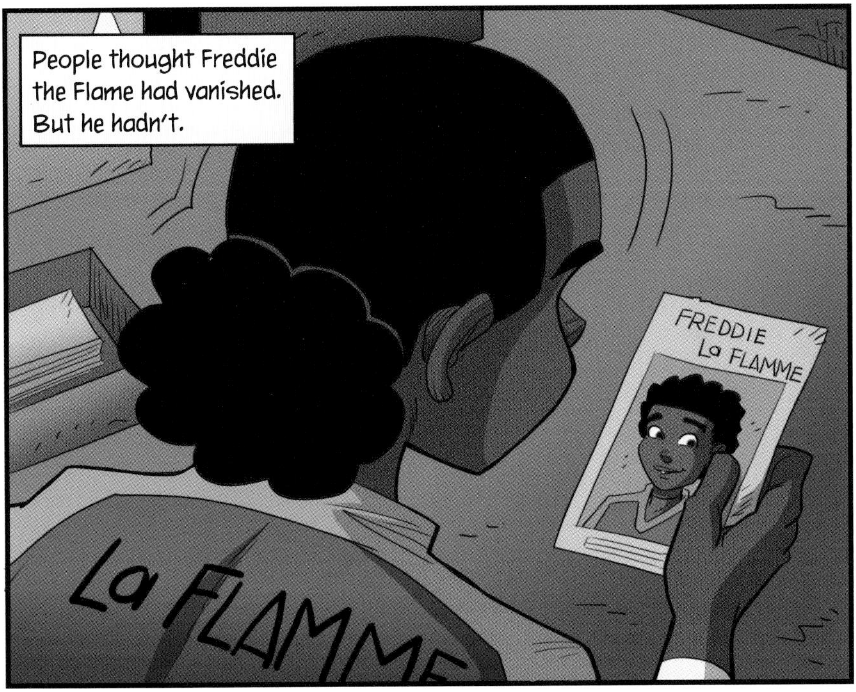
People thought Freddie the Flame had vanished. But he hadn't.
FREDDIE La FLAMME
La FLAMME

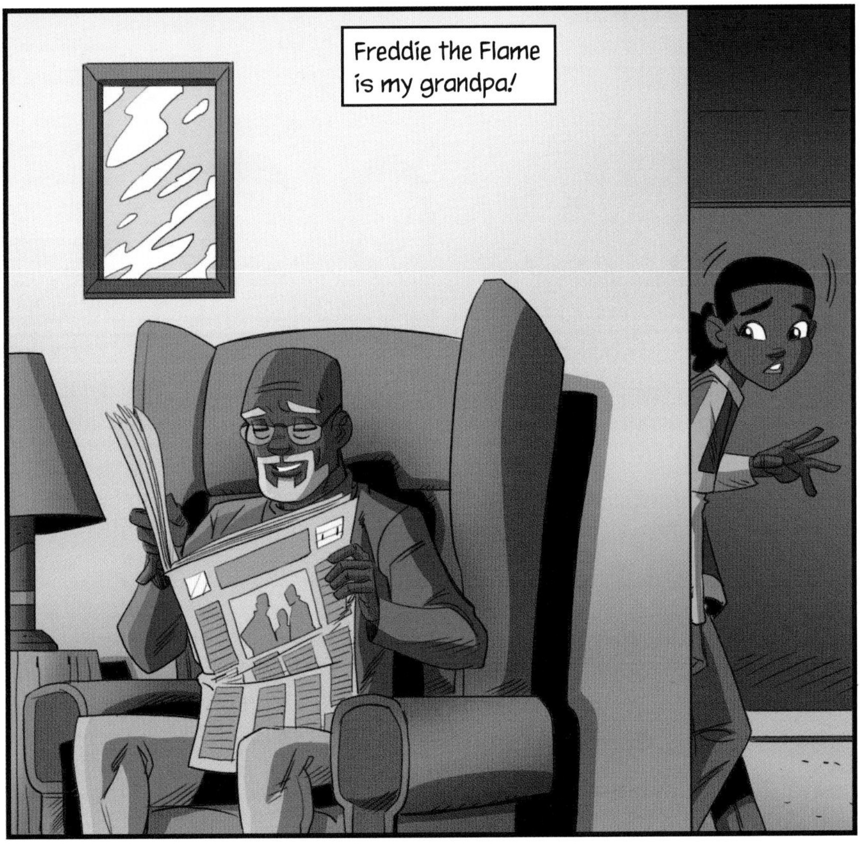
Freddie the Flame is my grandpa!

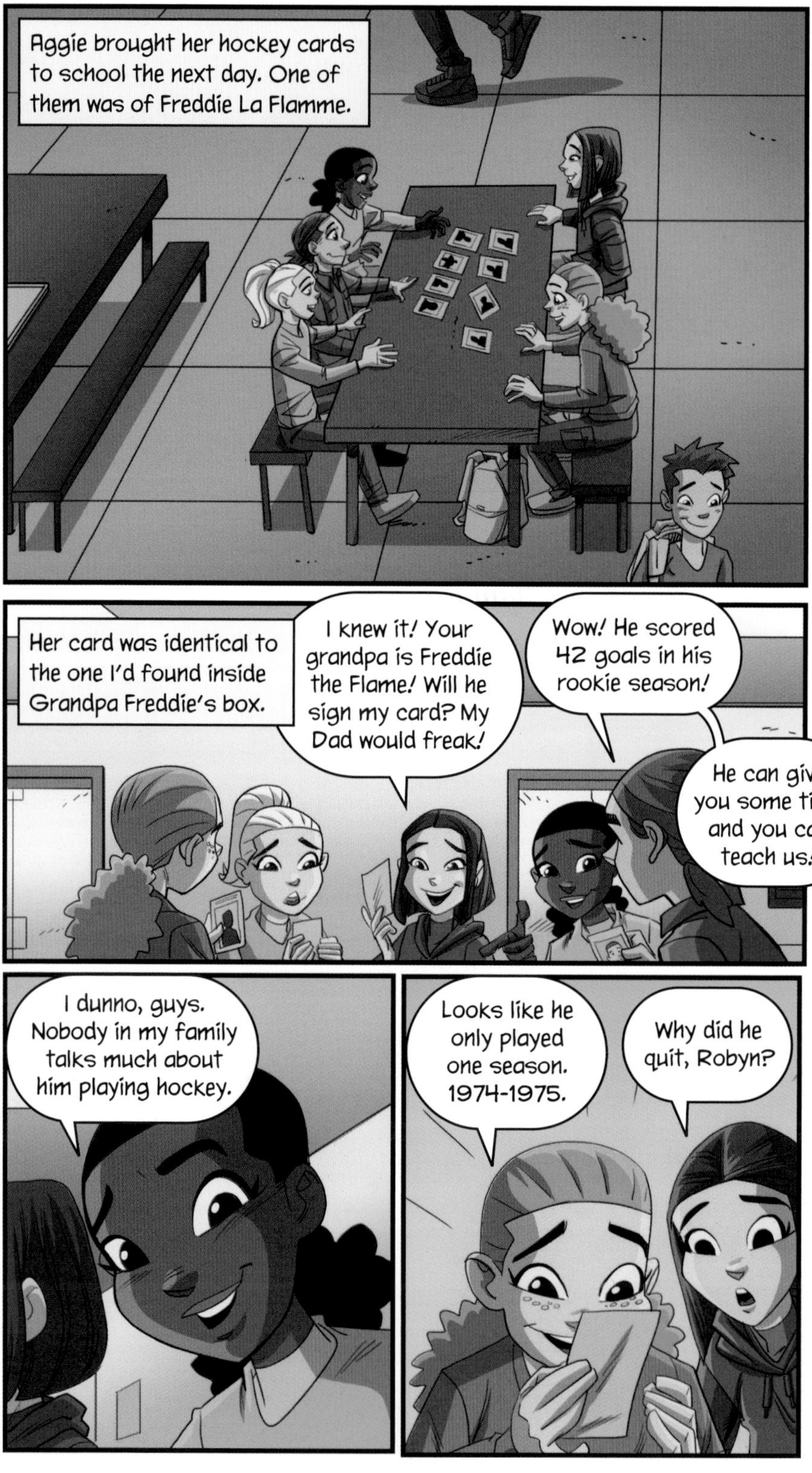
Aggie brought her hockey cards to school the next day. One of them was of Freddie La Flamme.
Her card was identical to the one I'd found inside Grandpa Freddie's box.
I knew it! Your grandpa is Freddie the Flame! Will he sign my card? My Dad would freak!
Wow! He scored 42 goals in his rookie season!
He can give you some tips, and you can teach us!
I dunno, guys. Nobody in my family talks much about him playing hockey.
Looks like he only played one season. 1974-1975.
Why did he quit, Robyn?

You really believe that Robyn's grandpa played professional hockey?

What's not to believe?

I don't know. You'd think Robyn wouldn't miss the net all the time if her grandpa was a pro hockey player!

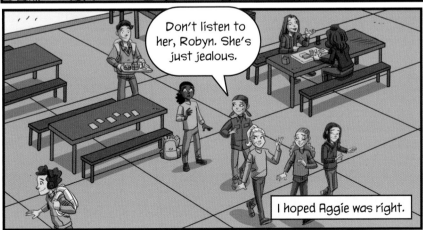

Don't listen to her, Robyn. She's just jealous.

I hoped Aggie was right.

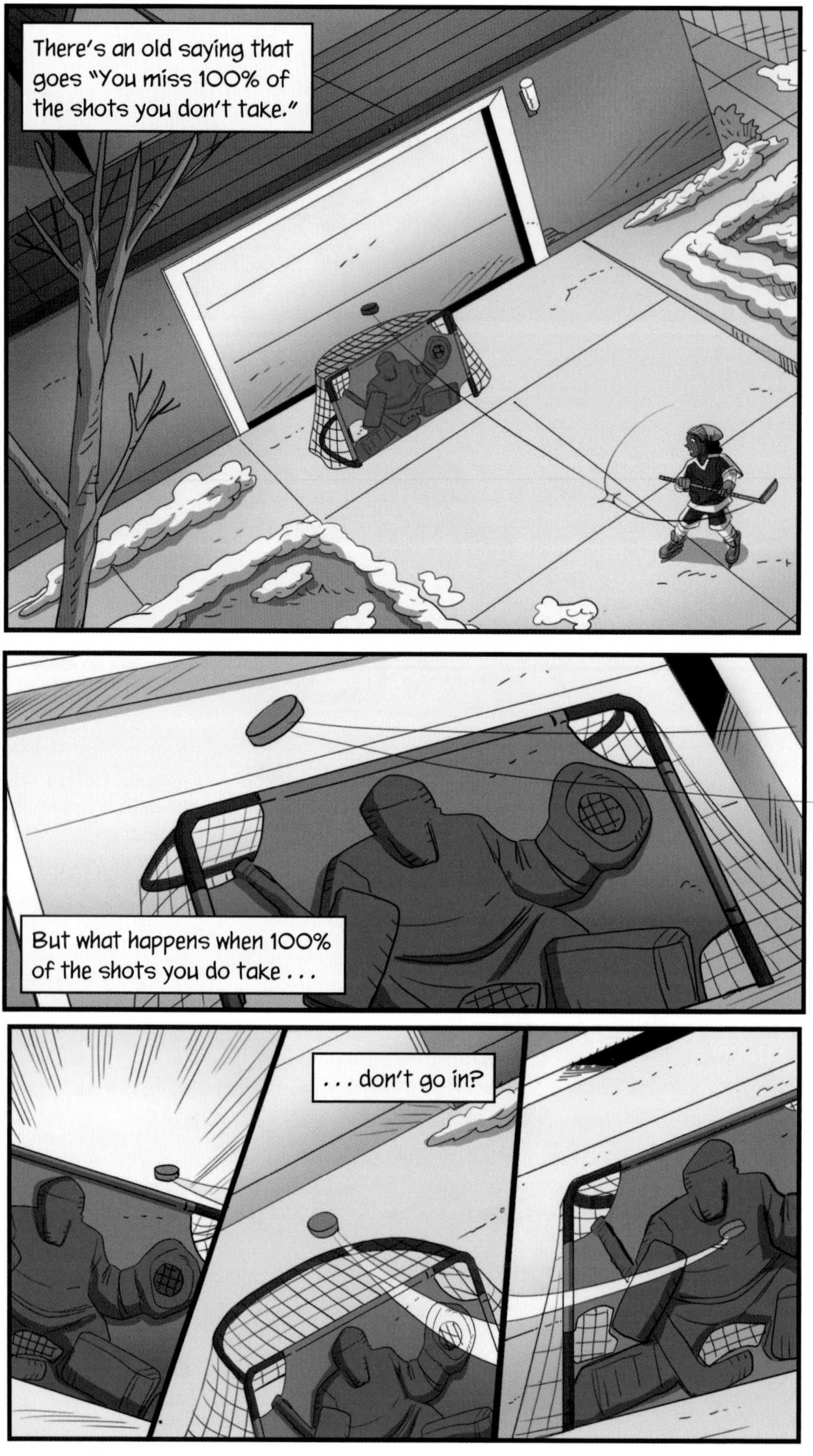
There's an old saying that goes "You miss 100% of the shots you don't take."
But what happens when 100% of the shots you do take . . .
. . . don't go in?

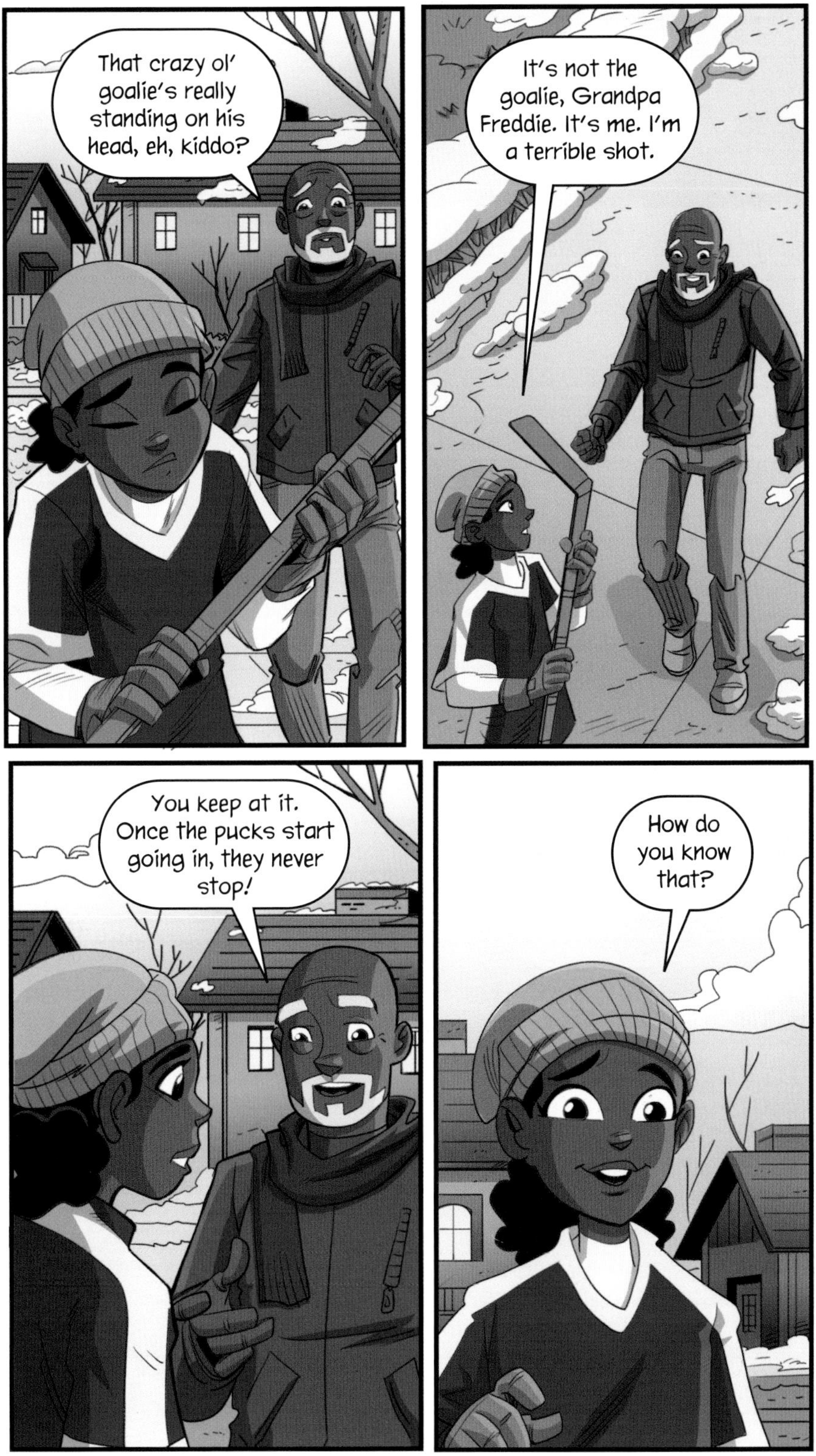
That crazy ol' goalie's really standing on his head, eh, kiddo?
It's not the goalie, Grandpa Freddie. It's me. I'm a terrible shot.
You keep at it. Once the pucks start going in, they never stop!
How do you know that?

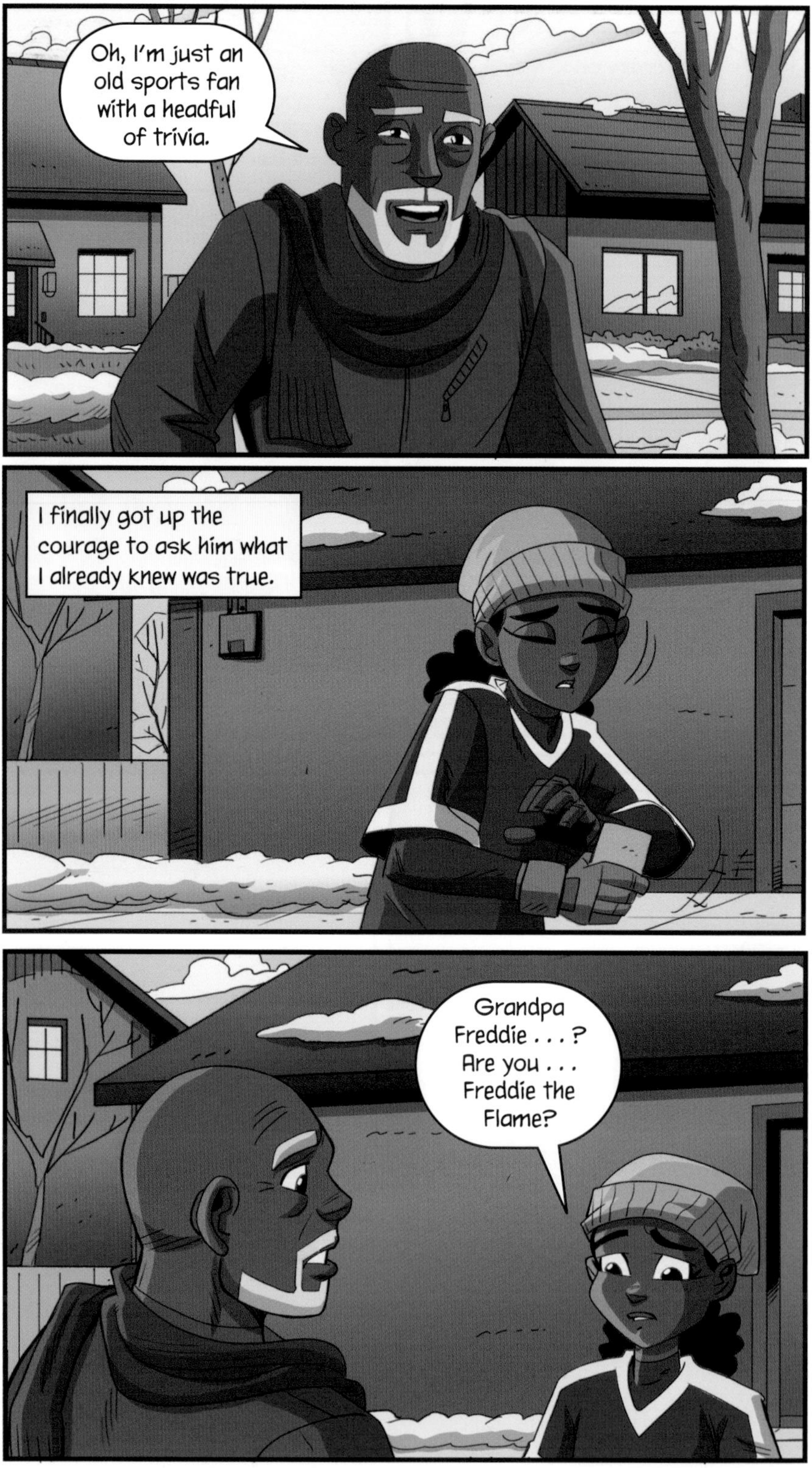
Oh, I'm just an old sports fan with a headful of trivia.
I finally got up the courage to ask him what I already knew was true.
Grandpa Freddie . . . ? Are you . . . Freddie the Flame?

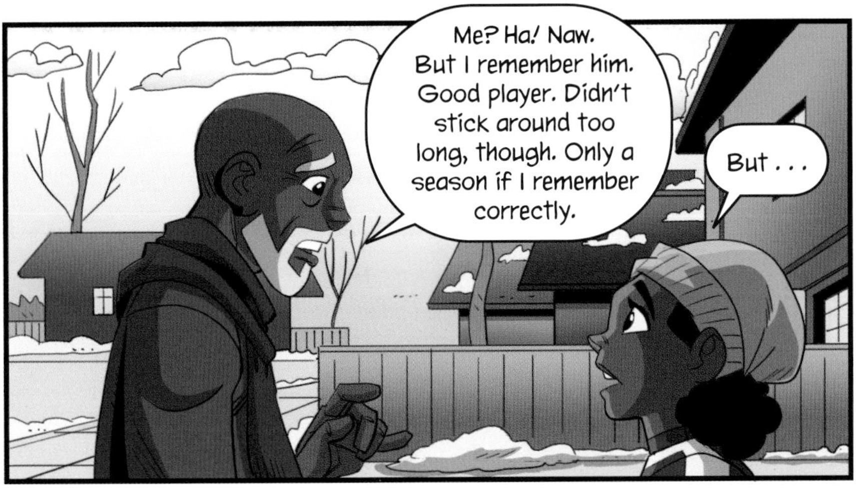
Me? Ha! Naw. But I remember him. Good player. Didn't stick around too long, though. Only a season if I remember correctly.
But . . .

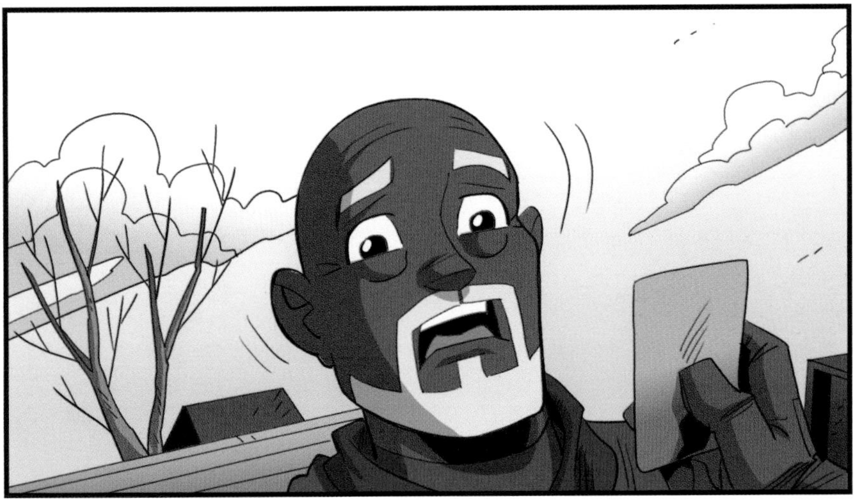

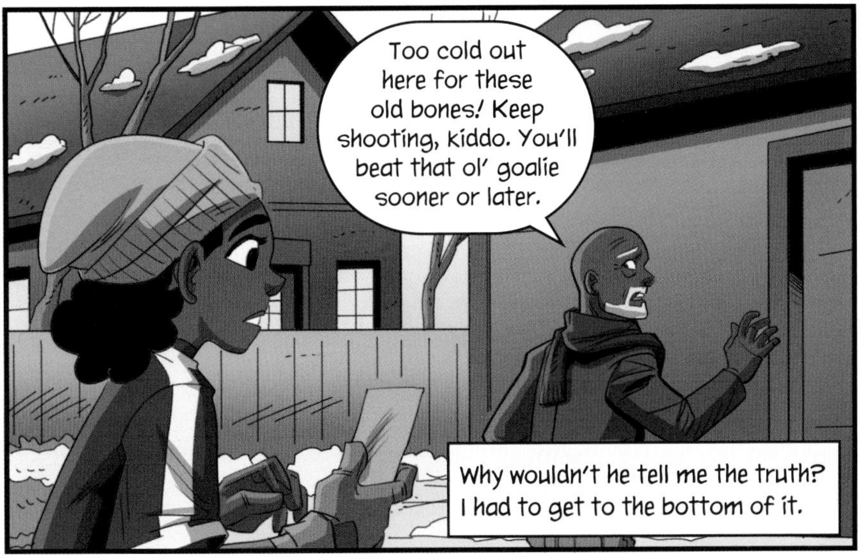
Too cold out here for these old bones! Keep shooting, kiddo. You'll beat that ol' goalie sooner or later.
Why wouldn't he tell me the truth? I had to get to the bottom of it.

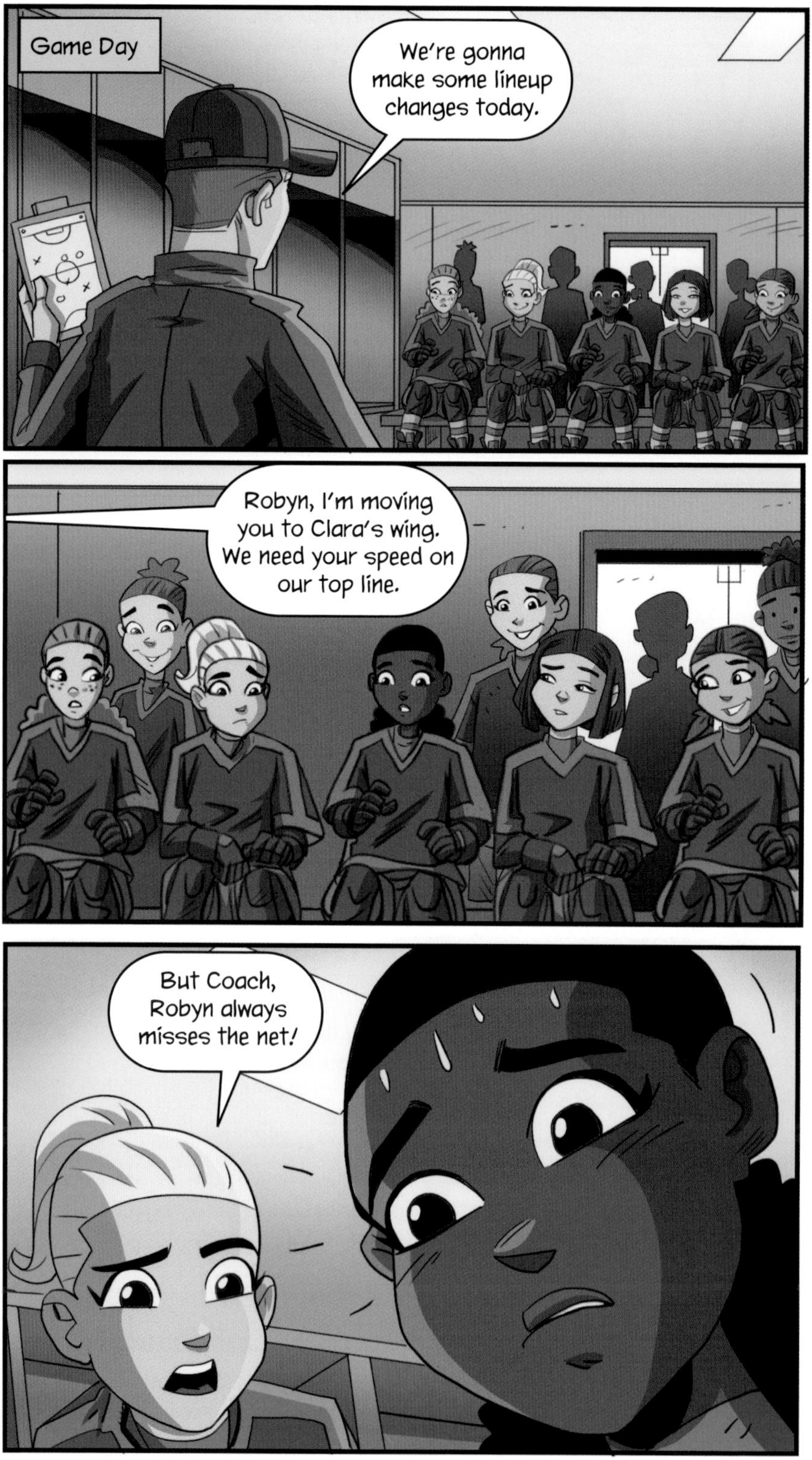
Game Day
We're gonna make some lineup changes today.
Robyn, I'm moving you to Clara's wing. We need your speed on our top line.
But Coach, Robyn always misses the net!

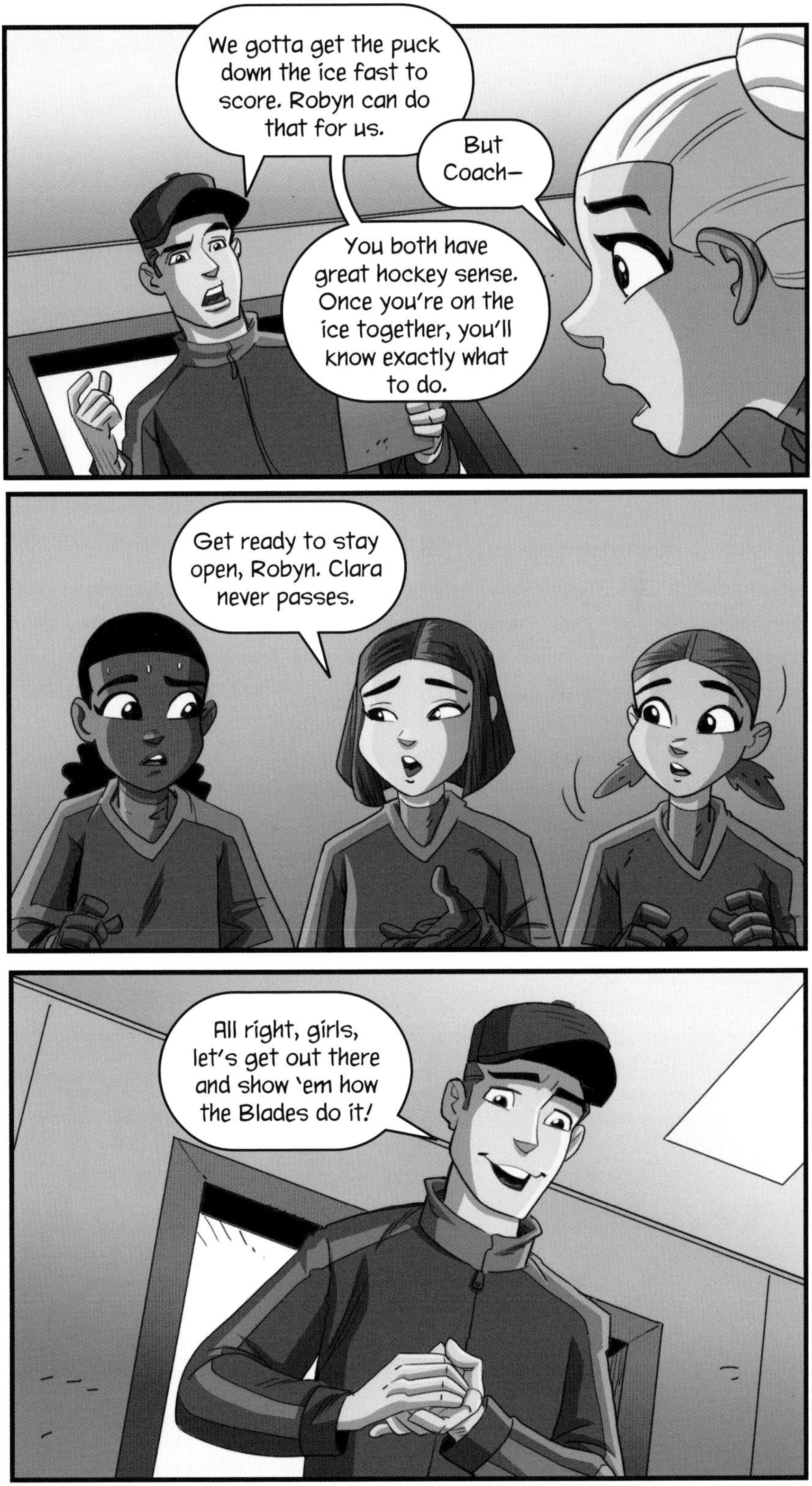
We gotta get the puck down the ice fast to score. Robyn can do that for us.
But Coach–
You both have great hockey sense. Once you're on the ice together, you'll know exactly what to do.
Get ready to stay open, Robyn. Clara never passes.
All right, girls, let's get out there and show 'em how the Blades do it!

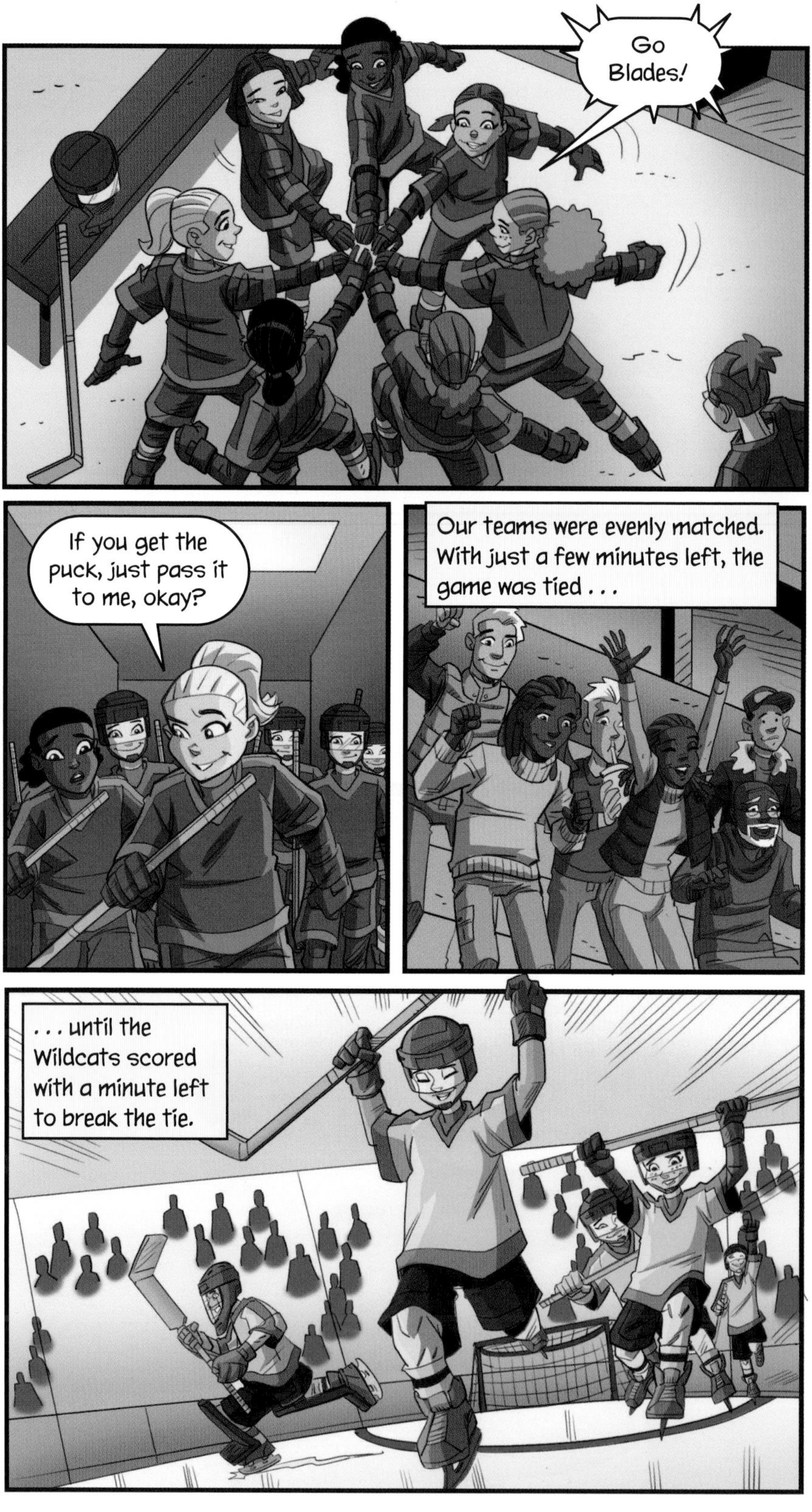
Go Blades!
If you get the puck, just pass it to me, okay?
Our teams were evenly matched. With just a few minutes left, the game was tied . . .
. . . until the Wildcats scored with a minute left to break the tie.

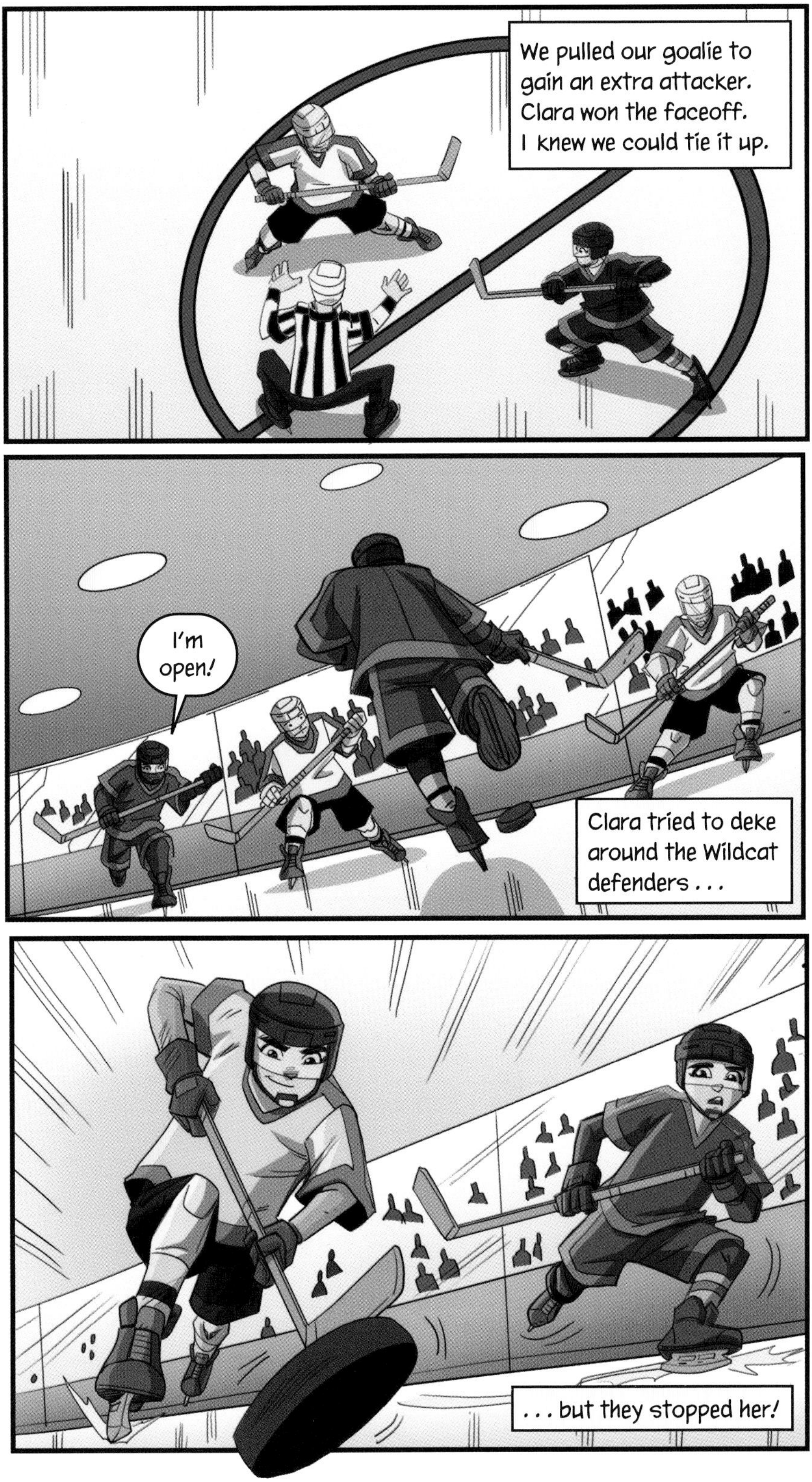
We pulled our goalie to gain an extra attacker. Clara won the faceoff. I knew we could tie it up.
I'm open!
Clara tried to deke around the Wildcat defenders . . .
. . . but they stopped her!

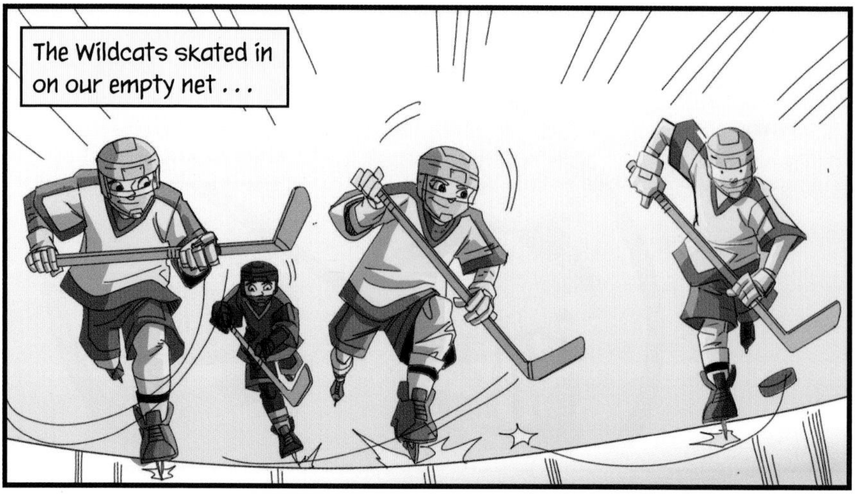
The Wildcats skated in on our empty net . . .

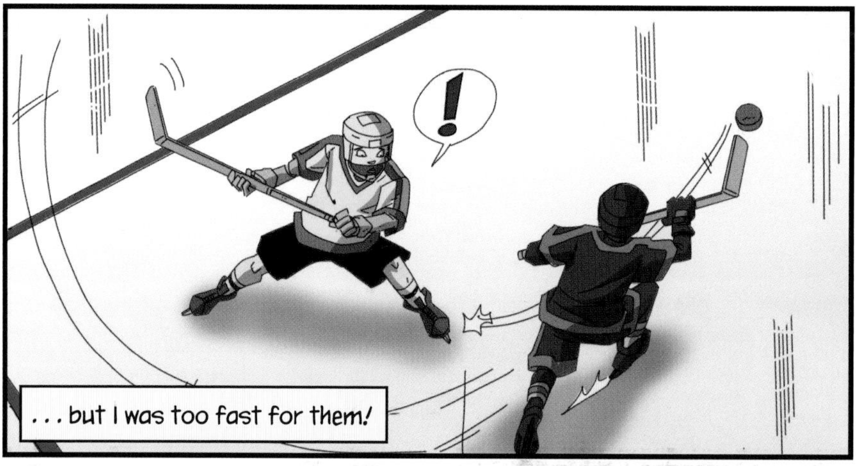
!
. . . but I was too fast for them!

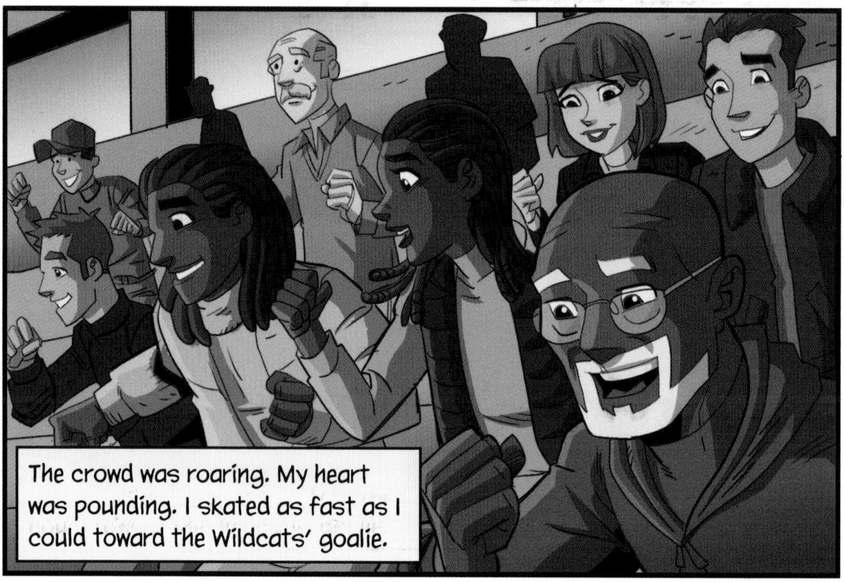
The crowd was roaring. My heart was pounding. I skated as fast as I could toward the Wildcats' goalie.

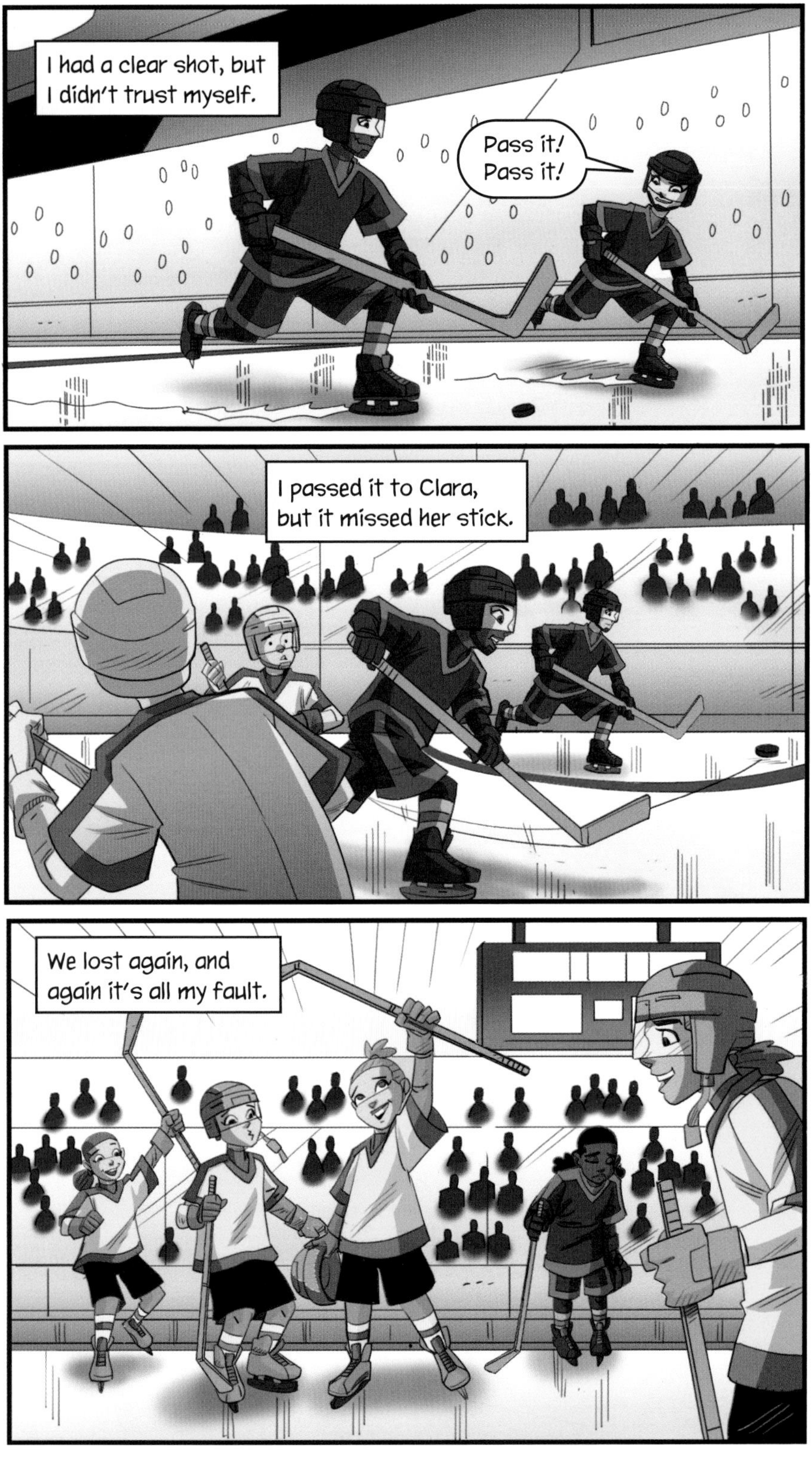
I had a clear shot, but I didn't trust myself.
Pass it! Pass it!
I passed it to Clara, but it missed her stick.
We lost again, and again it's all my fault.

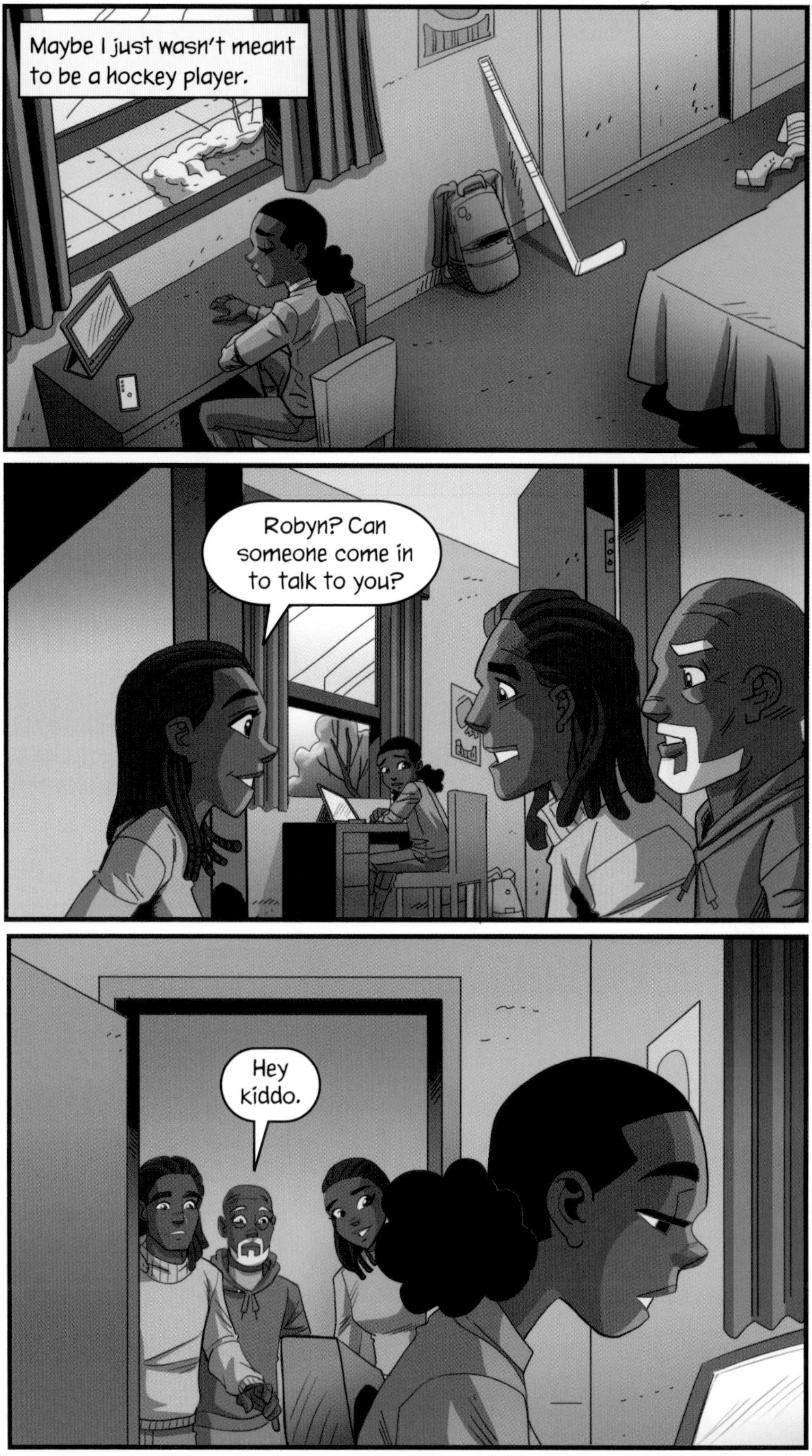
Maybe I just wasn't meant to be a hockey player.
Robyn? Can someone come in to talk to you?
Hey kiddo.

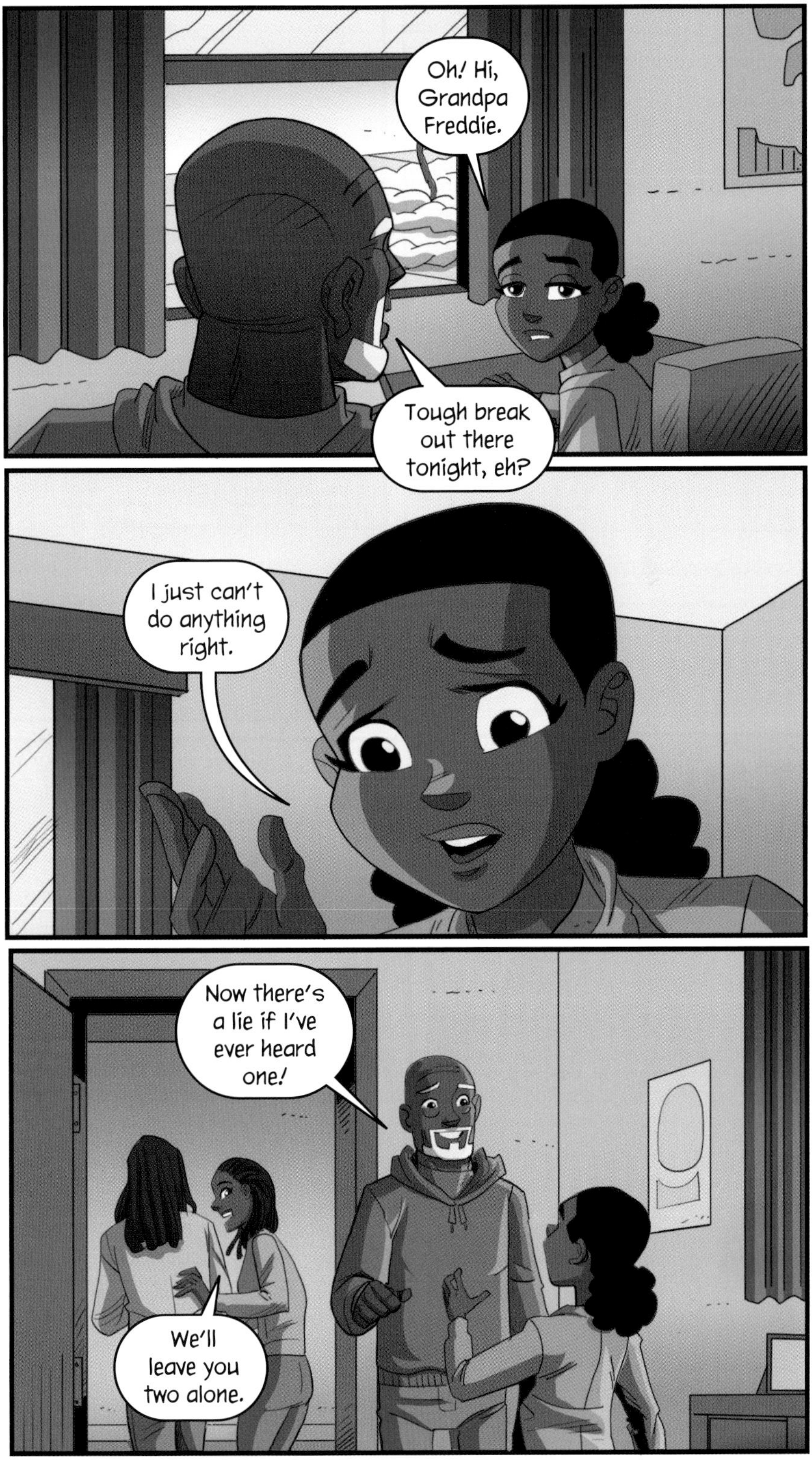
Oh! Hi, Grandpa Freddie.
Tough break out there tonight, eh?
I just can't do anything right.
Now there's a lie if I've ever heard one!
We'll leave you two alone.

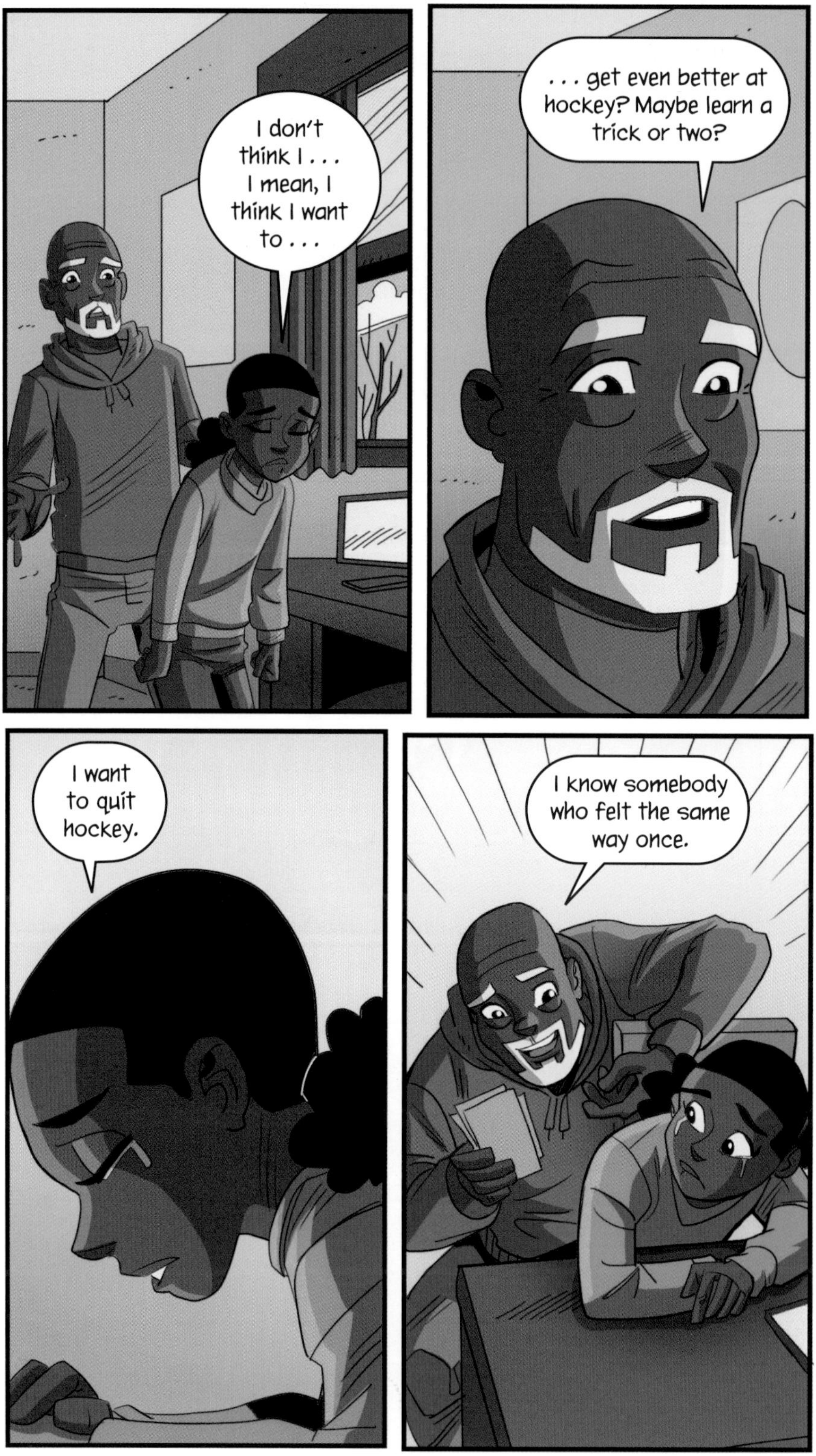
I don't think I . . . I mean, I think I want to . . .
. . . get even better at hockey? Maybe learn a trick or two?
I want to quit hockey.
I know somebody who felt the same way once.

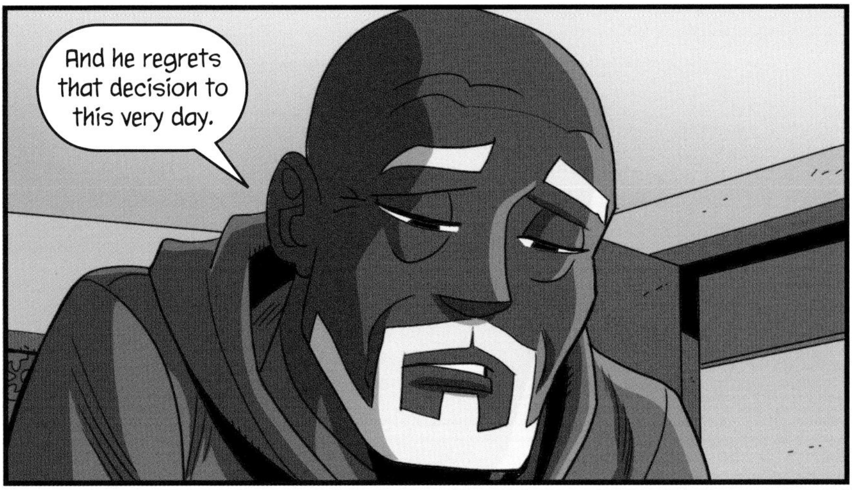
And he regrets that decision to this very day.

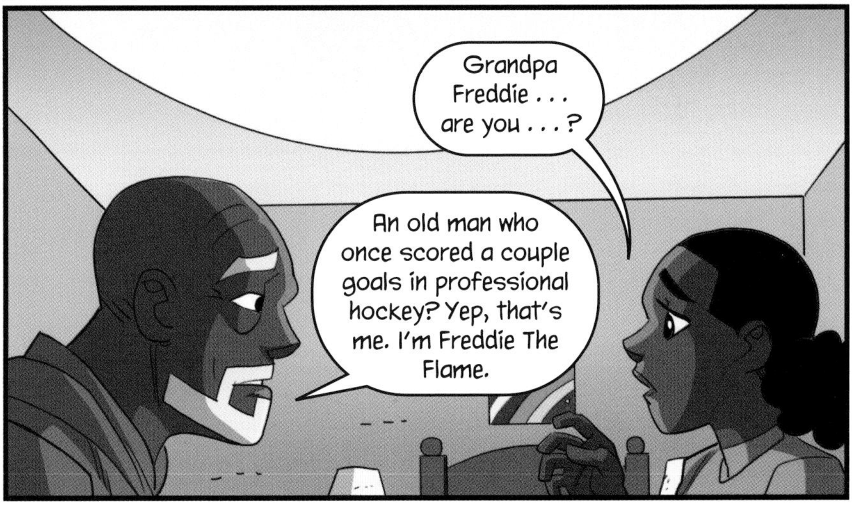
Grandpa Freddie . . . are you . . . ?
An old man who once scored a couple goals in professional hockey? Yep, that's me. I'm Freddie The Flame.

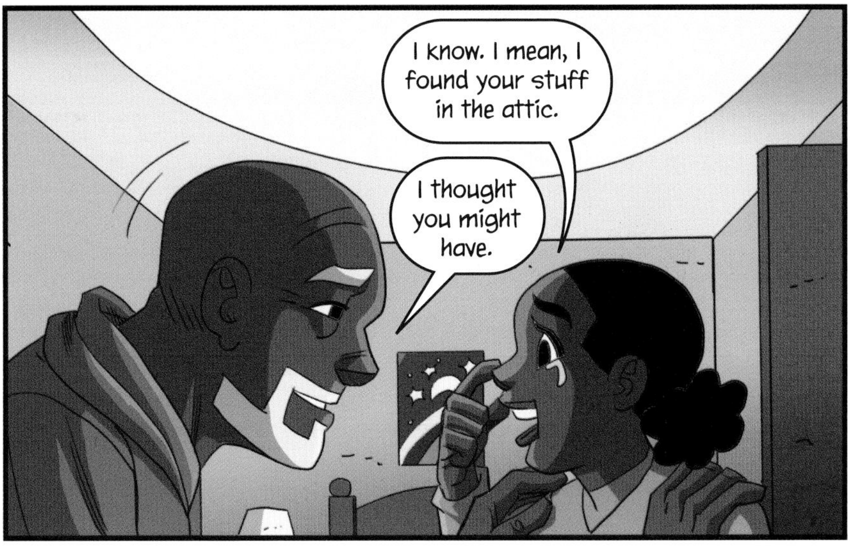
I know. I mean, I found your stuff in the attic.
I thought you might have.

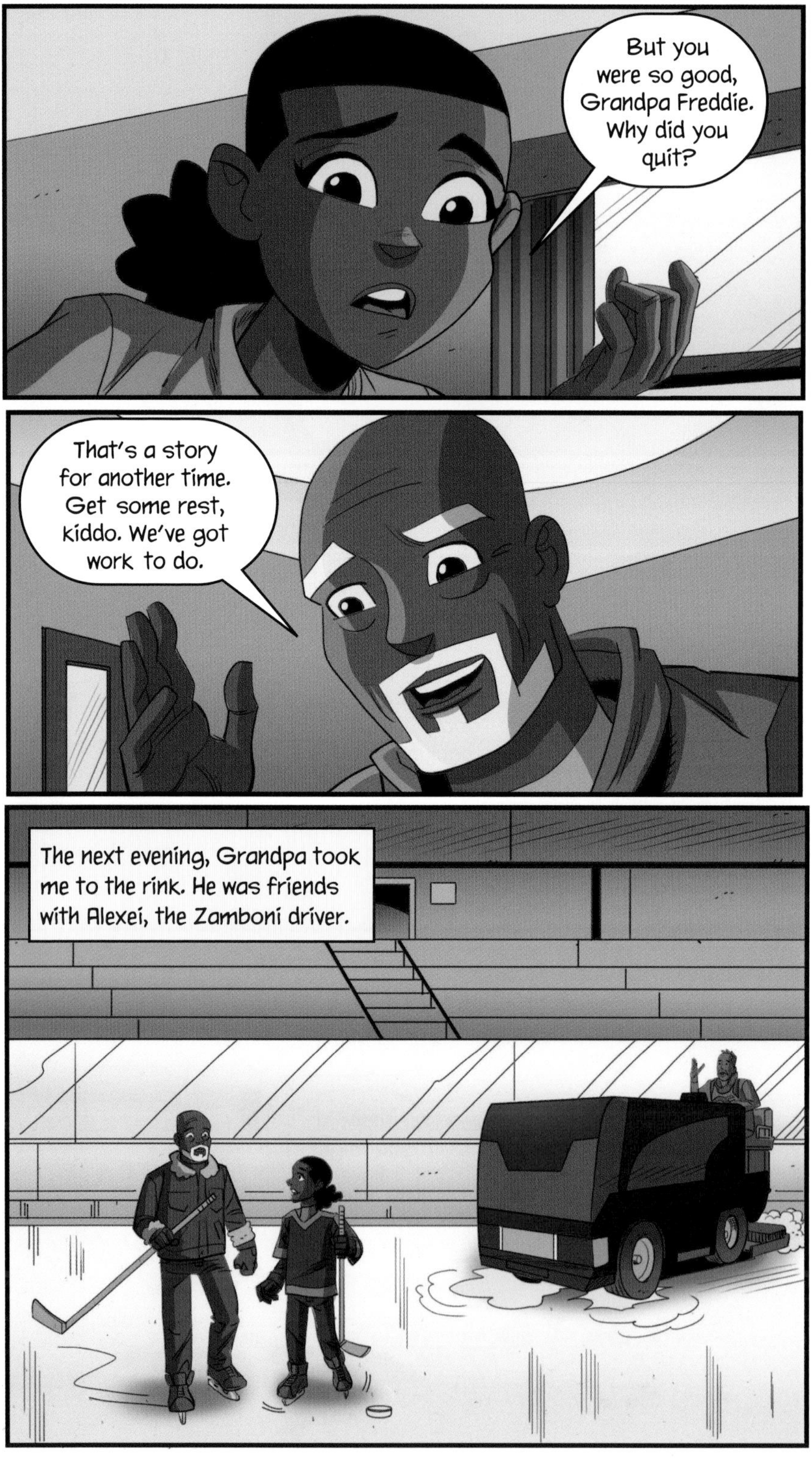

But you were so good, Grandpa Freddie. Why did you quit?
That's a story for another time. Get some rest, kiddo. We've got work to do.
The next evening, Grandpa took me to the rink. He was friends with Alexei, the Zamboni driver.

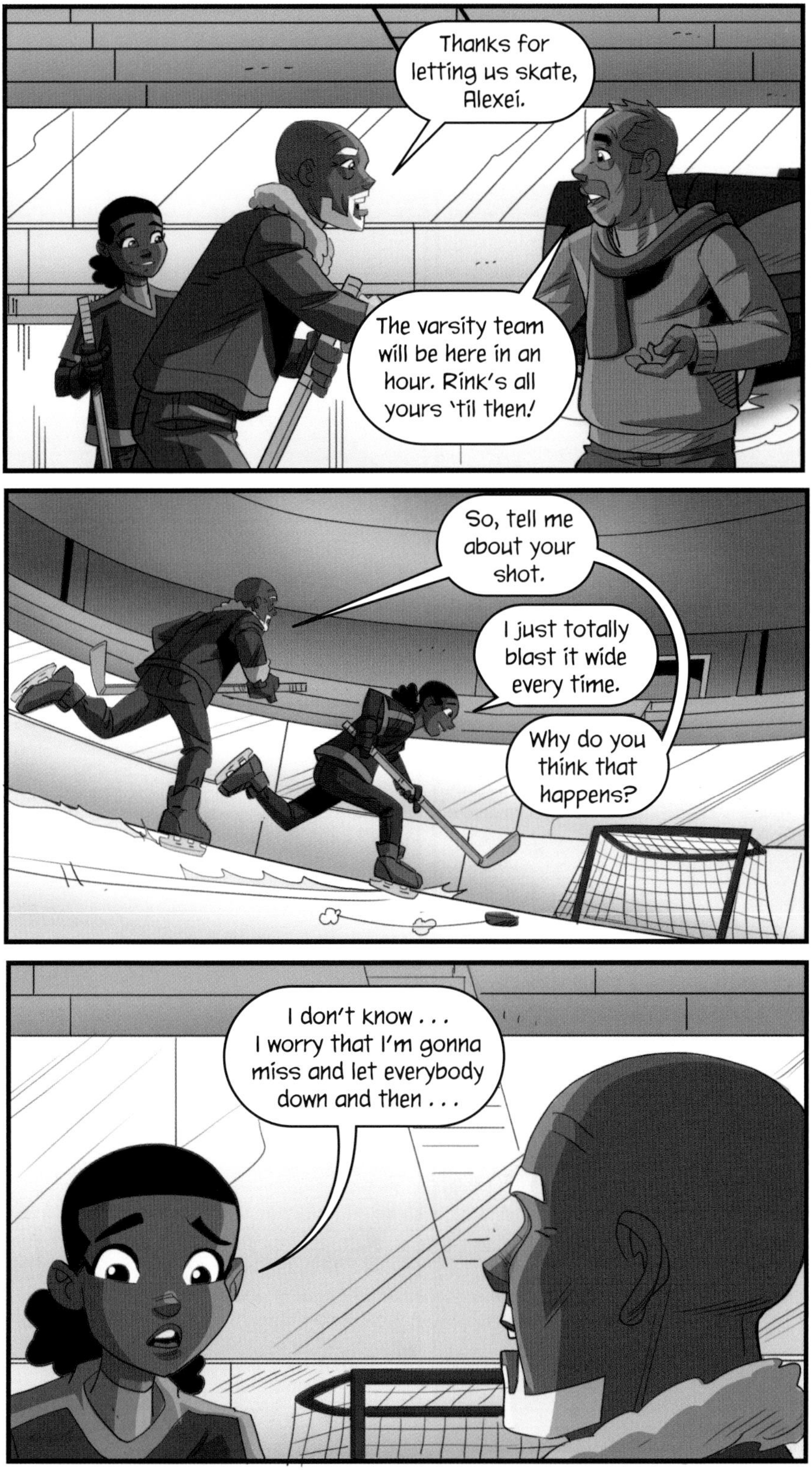
Thanks for letting us skate, Alexei.
The varsity team will be here in an hour. Rink's all yours 'til then!
So, tell me about your shot.
I just totally blast it wide every time.
Why do you think that happens?
I don't know . . . I worry that I'm gonna miss and let everybody down and then . . .

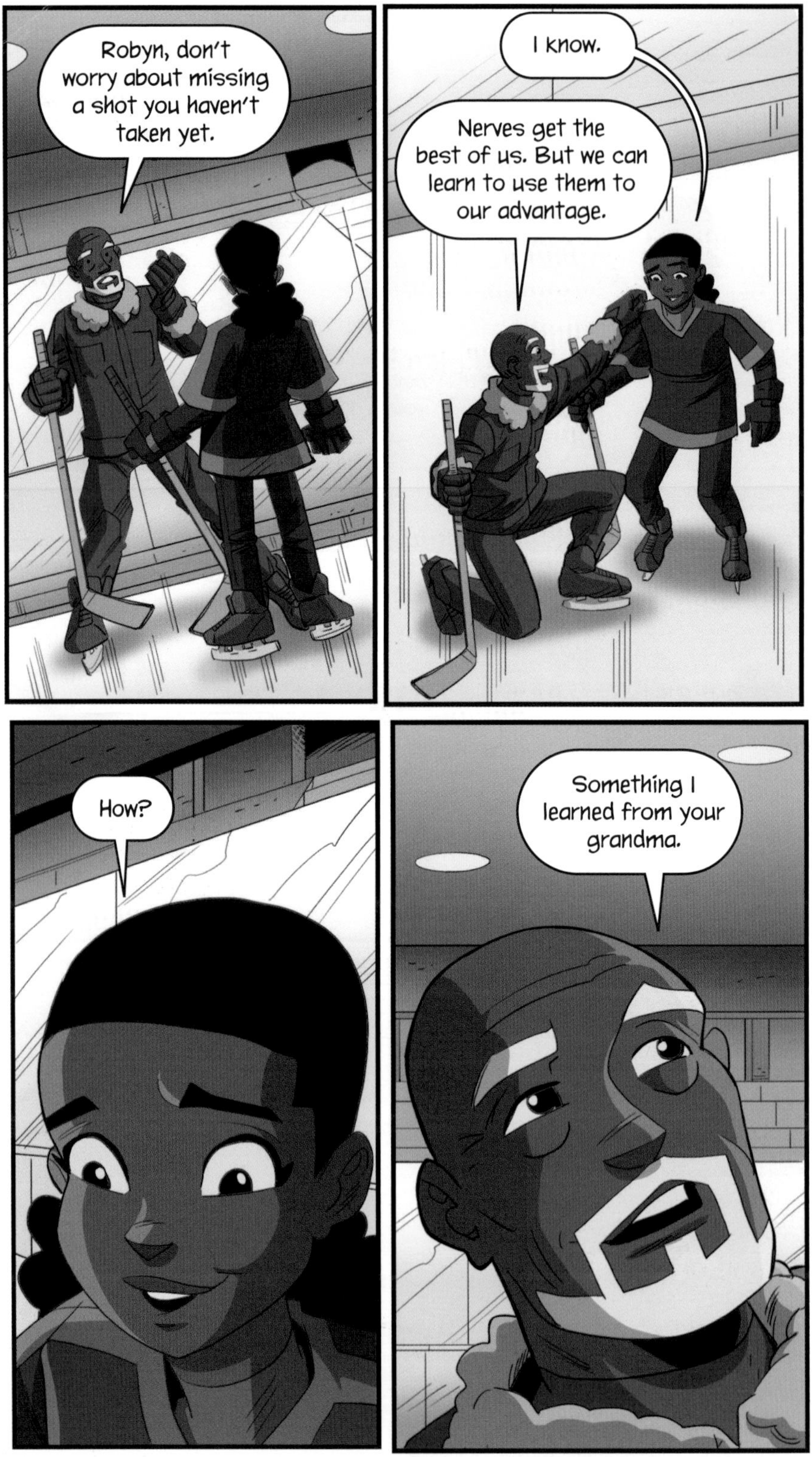
Robyn, don't worry about missing a shot you haven't taken yet.
I know.
Nerves get the best of us. But we can learn to use them to our advantage.
How?
Something I learned from your grandma.

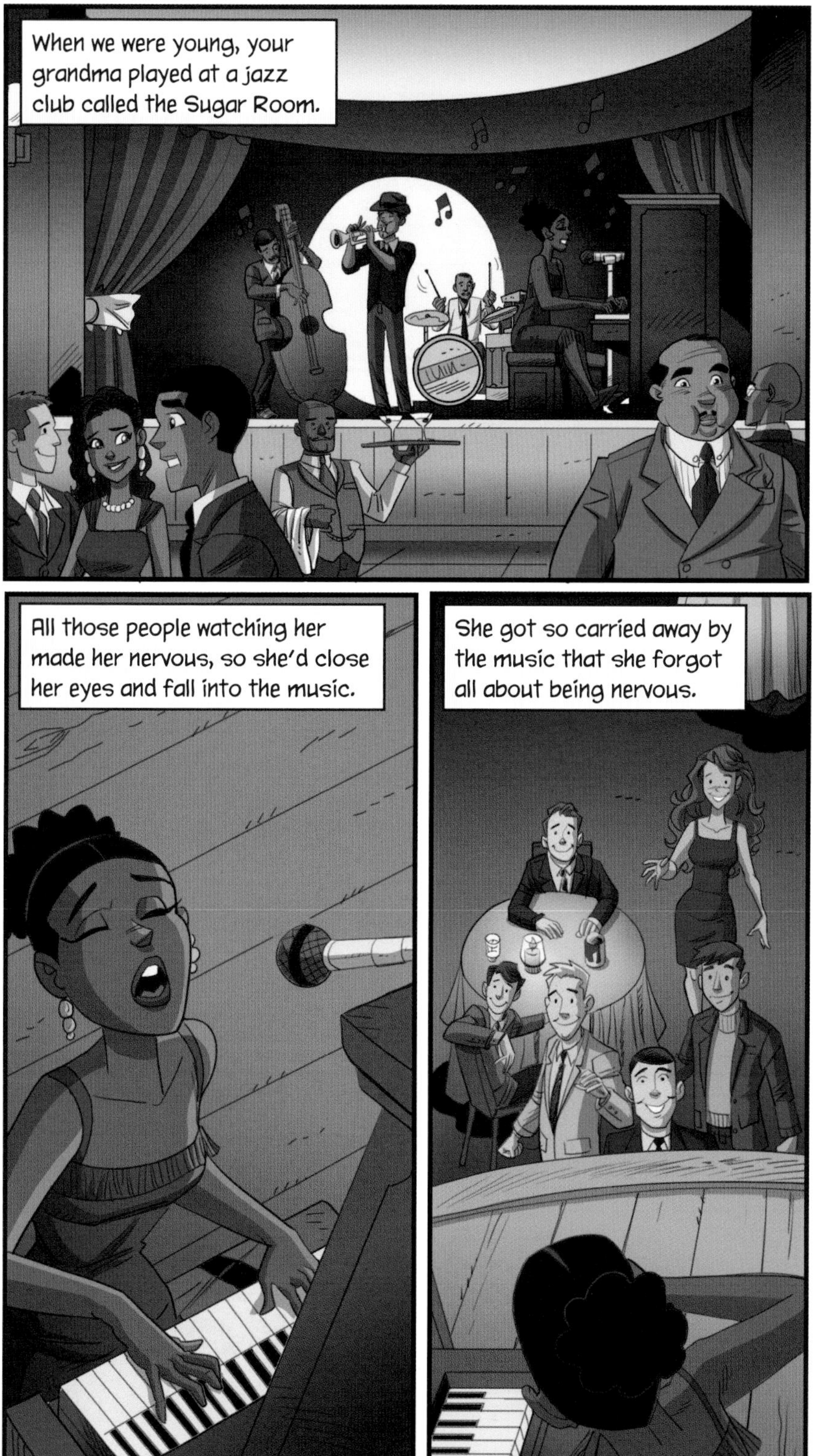
When we were young, your grandma played at a jazz club called the Sugar Room.
All those people watching her made her nervous, so she'd close her eyes and fall into the music.
She got so carried away by the music that she forgot all about being nervous.

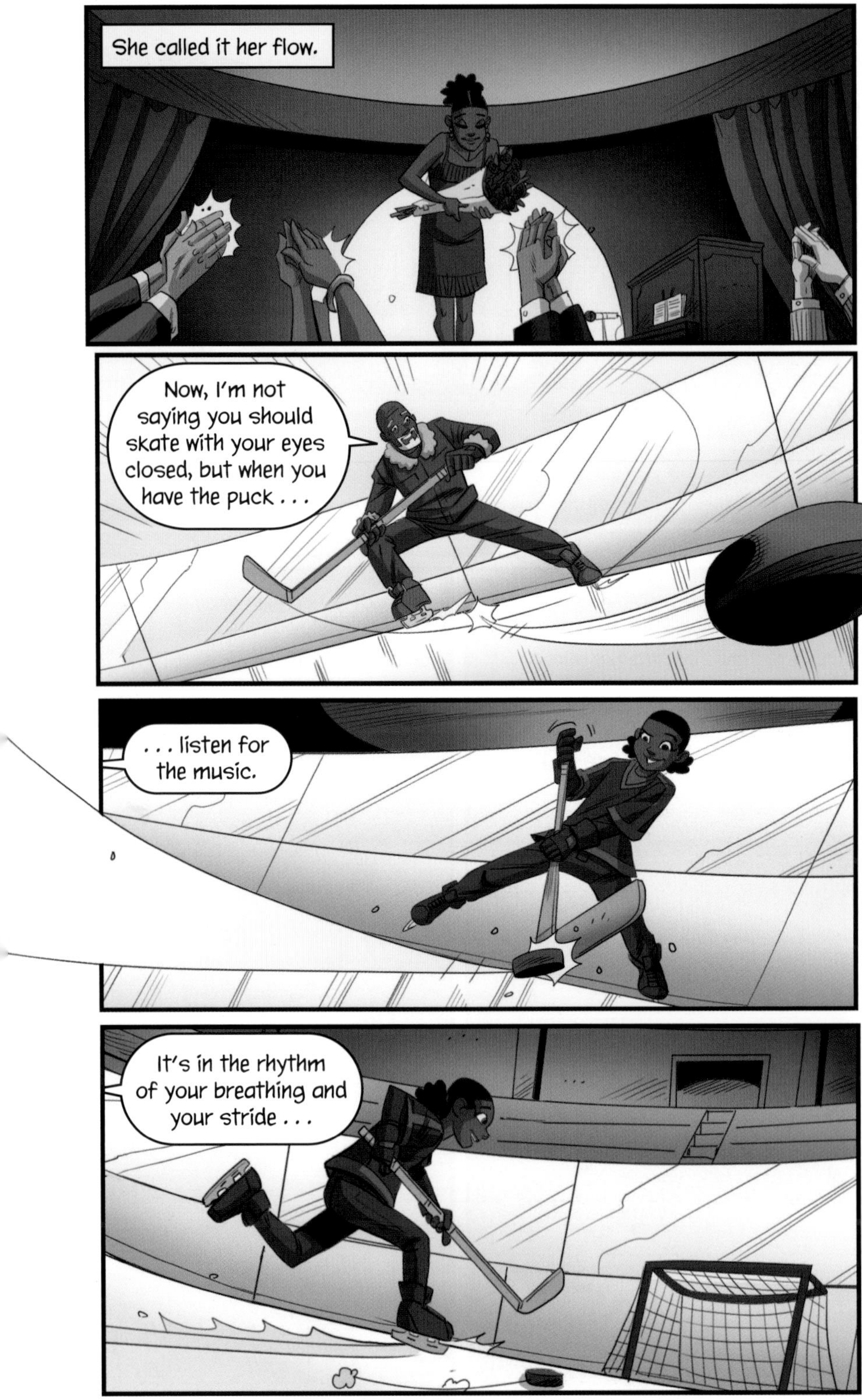
She called it her flow.
Now, I'm not saying you should skate with your eyes closed, but when you have the puck . . .
. . . listen for the music.
It's in the rhythm of your breathing and your stride . . .

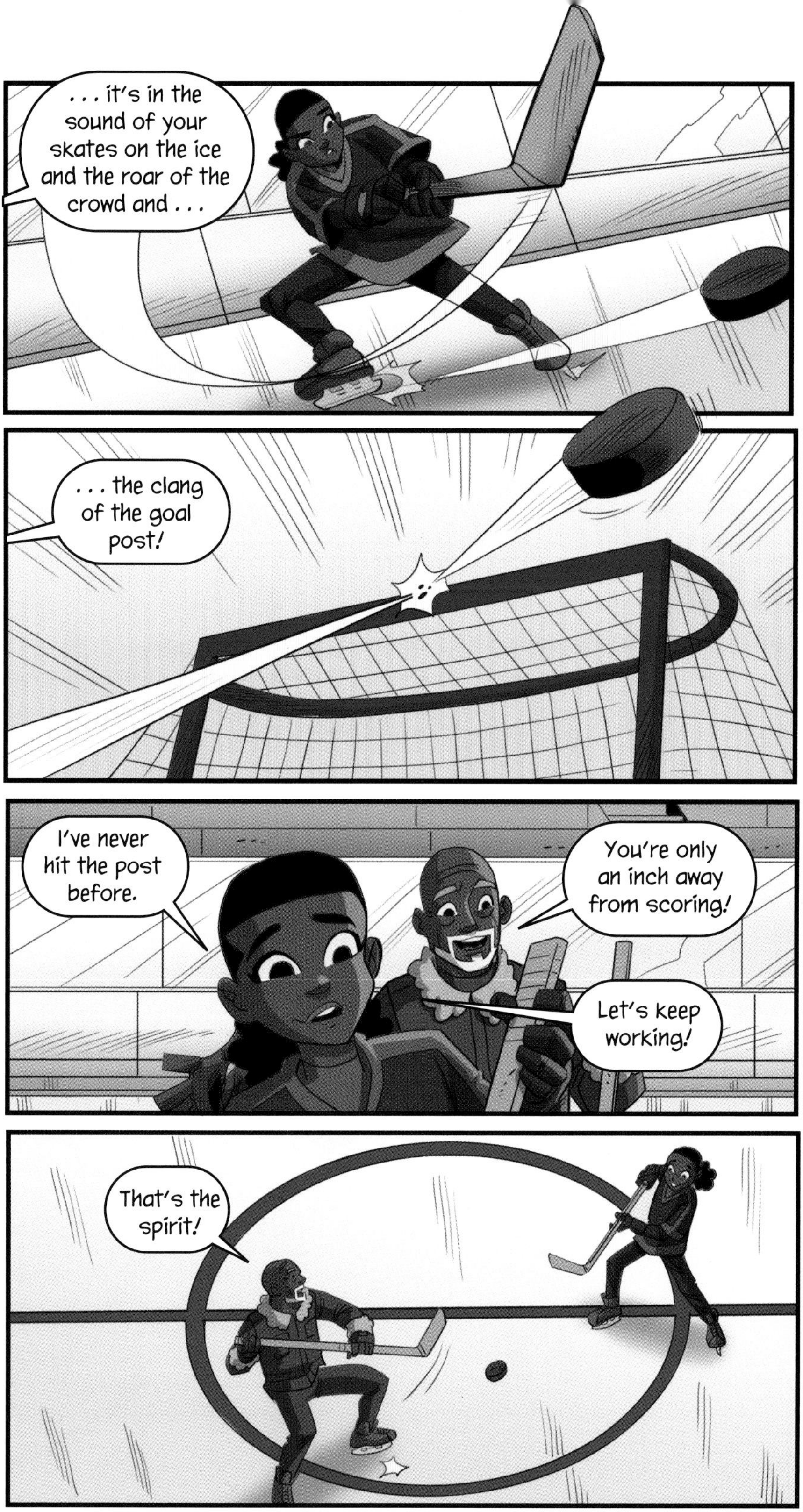

. . . it's in the sound of your skates on the ice and the roar of the crowd and . . .
. . . the clang of the goal post!
I've never hit the post before.
You're only an inch away from scoring!
Let's keep working!
That's the spirit!

Grandpa Freddie and I met each night at the rink to run more drills. His friend Alexei played goalie.

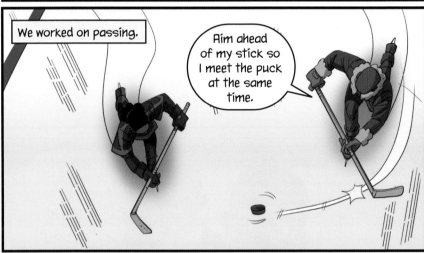

We worked on passing.

Aim ahead of my stick so I meet the puck at the same time.

We worked on wrist shots.

The wrister is all in the snap of your hands!

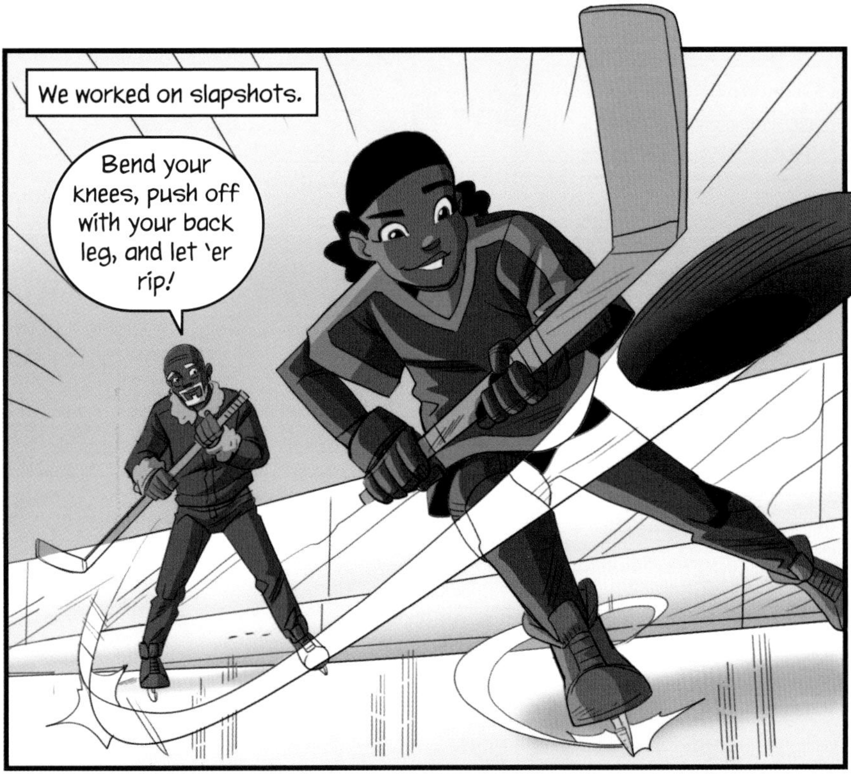
We worked on slapshots.
Bend your knees, push off with your back leg, and let 'er rip!

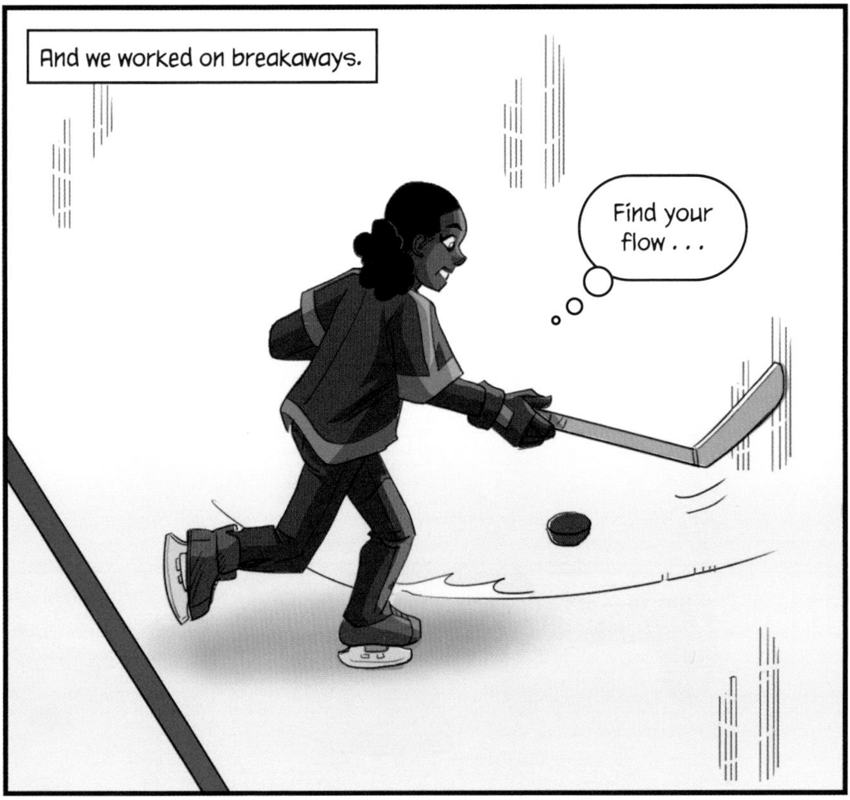
And we worked on breakaways.
Find your flow . . .

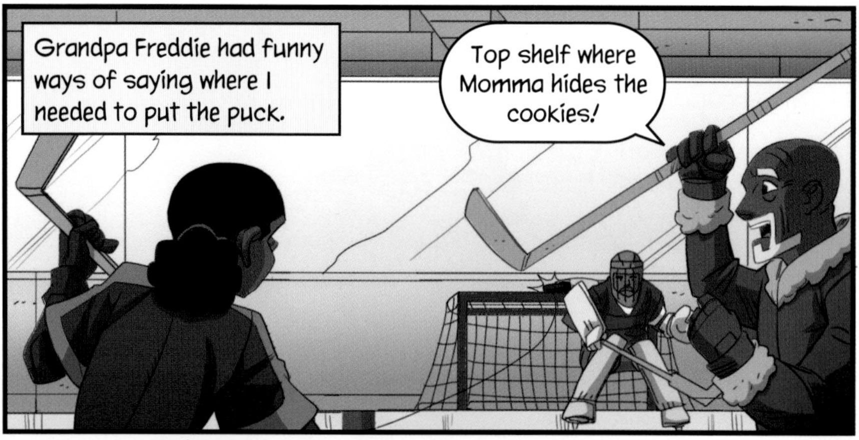
Grandpa Freddie had funny ways of saying where I needed to put the puck.
Top shelf where Momma hides the cookies!

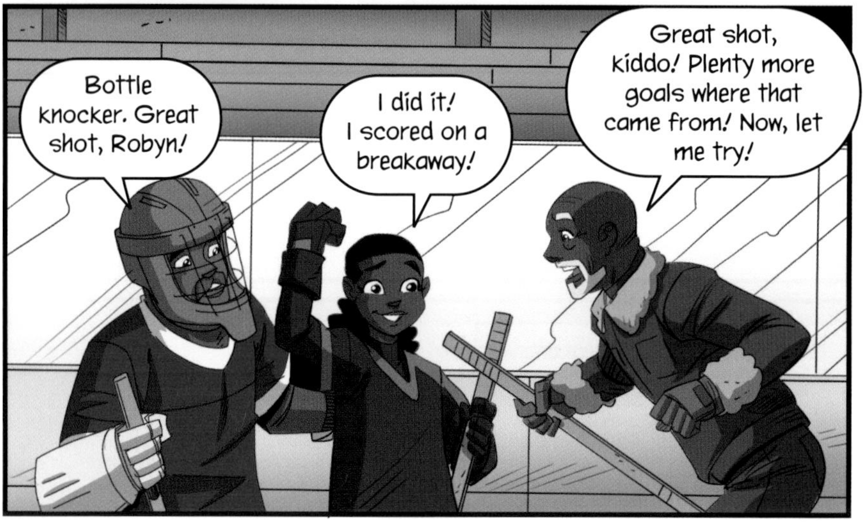
Bottle knocker. Great shot, Robyn!
I did it! I scored on a breakaway!
Great shot, kiddo! Plenty more goals where that came from! Now, let me try!

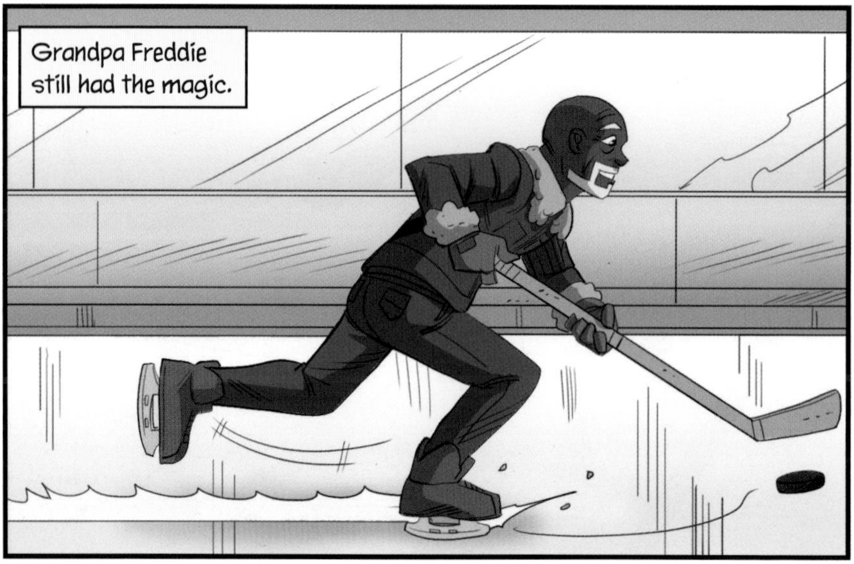
Grandpa Freddie still had the magic.

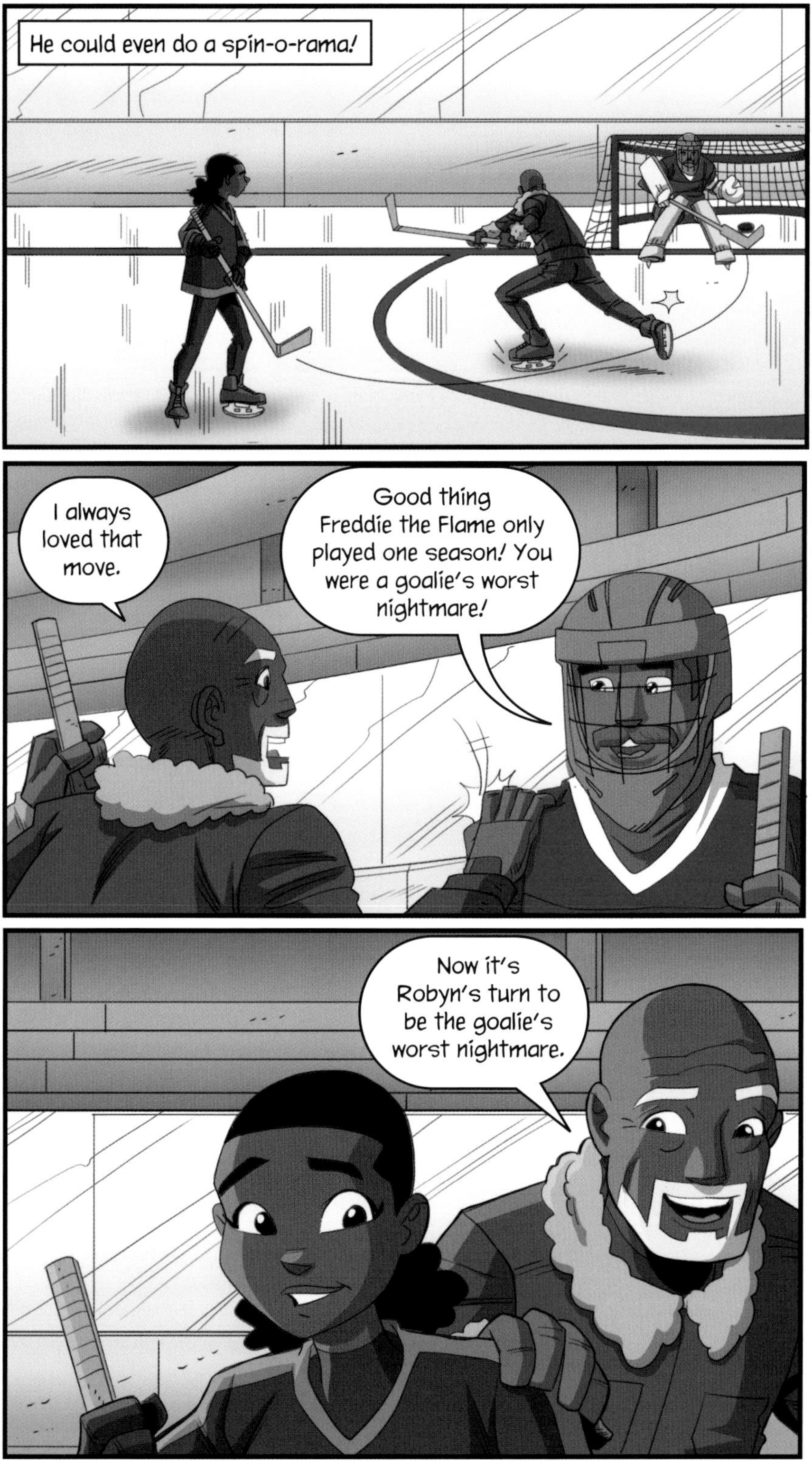
He could even do a spin-o-rama!
I always loved that move.
Good thing Freddie the Flame only played one season! You were a goalie's worst nightmare!
Now it's Robyn's turn to be the goalie's worst nightmare.

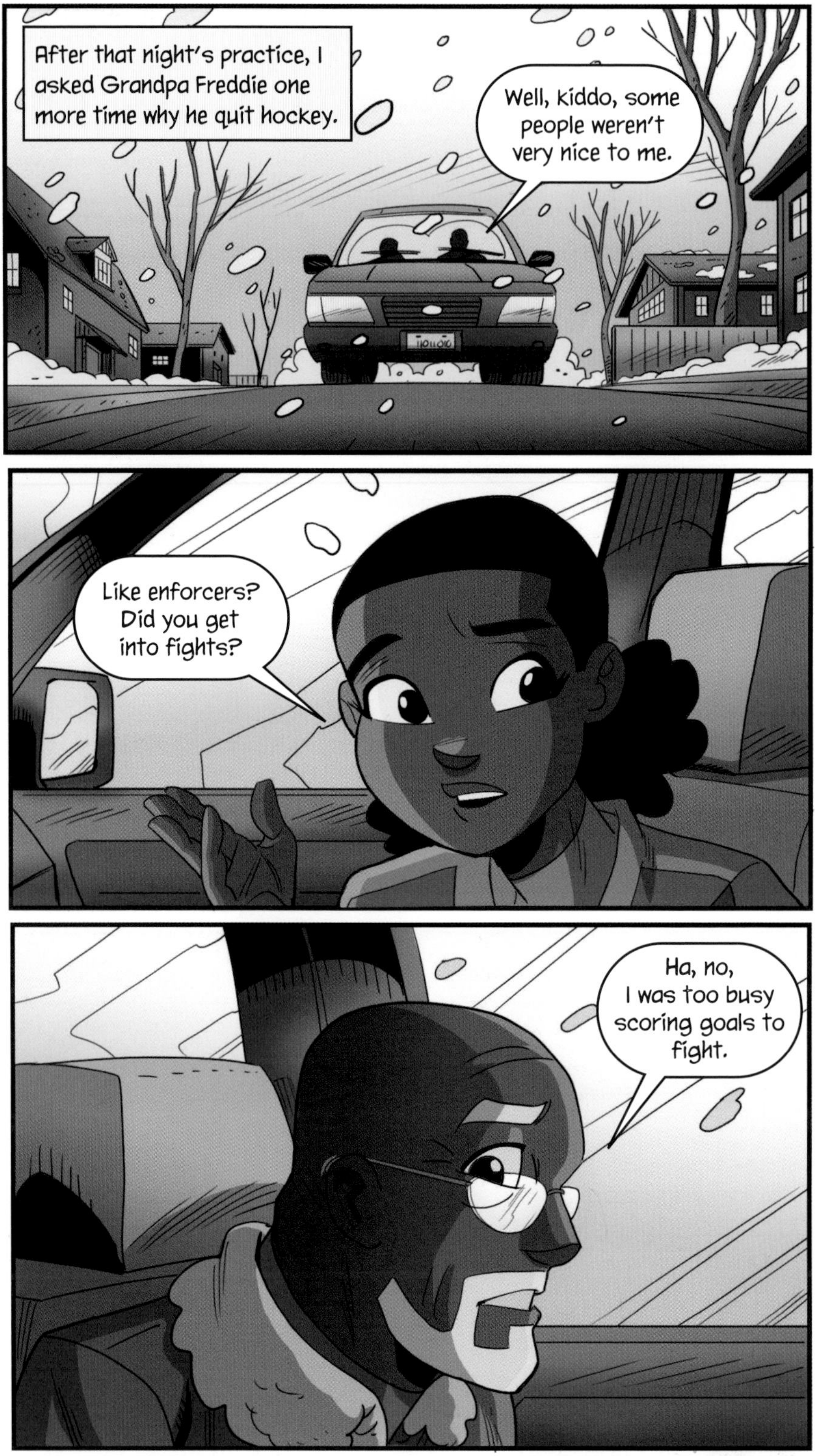
After that night's practice, I asked Grandpa Freddie one more time why he quit hockey.
Well, kiddo, some people weren't very nice to me.
Like enforcers? Did you get into fights?
Ha, no, I was too busy scoring goals to fight.

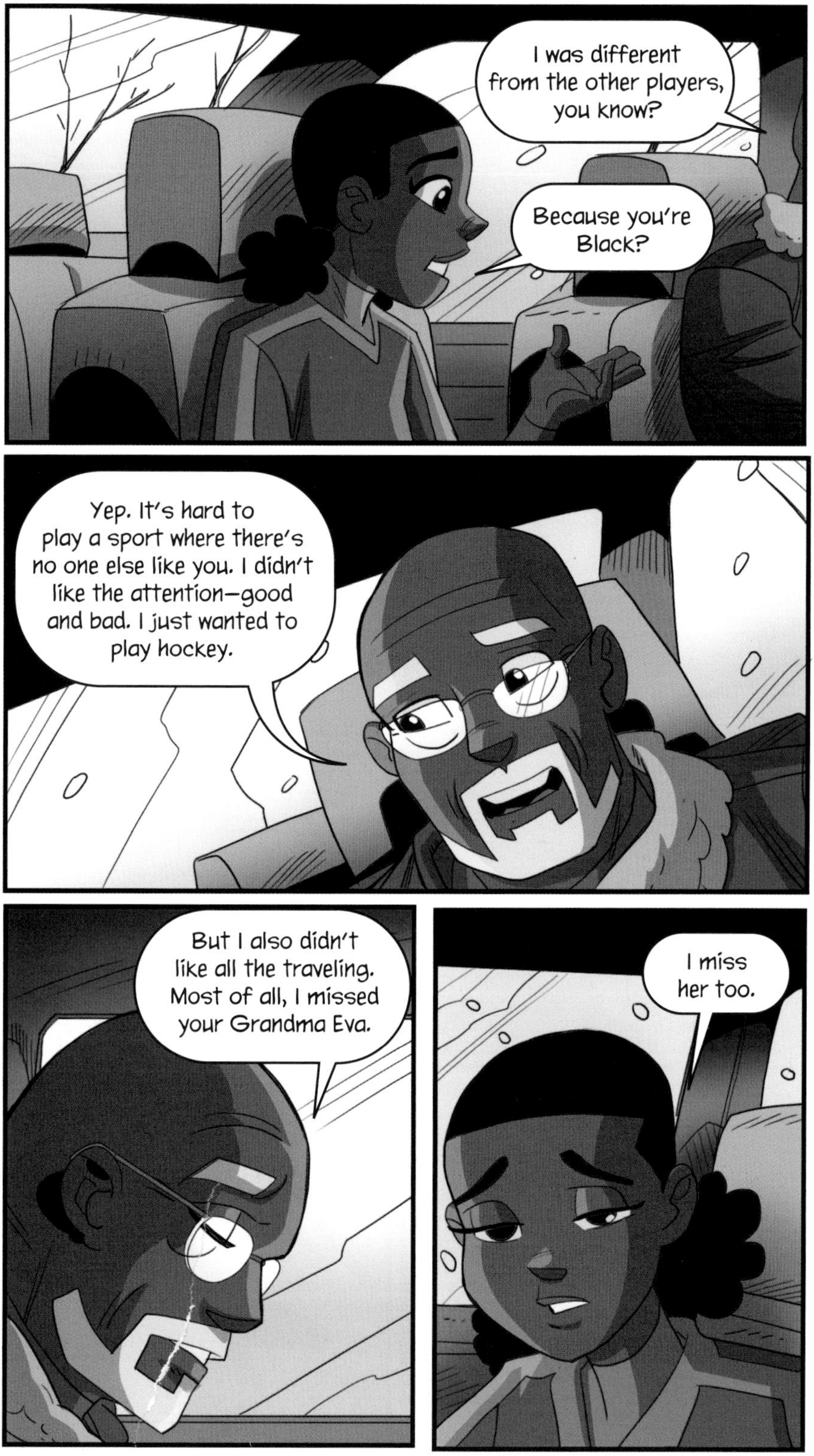
I was different from the other players, you know?
Because you're Black?
Yep. It's hard to play a sport where there's no one else like you. I didn't like the attention—good and bad. I just wanted to play hockey.
But I also didn't like all the traveling. Most of all, I missed your Grandma Eva.
I miss her too.

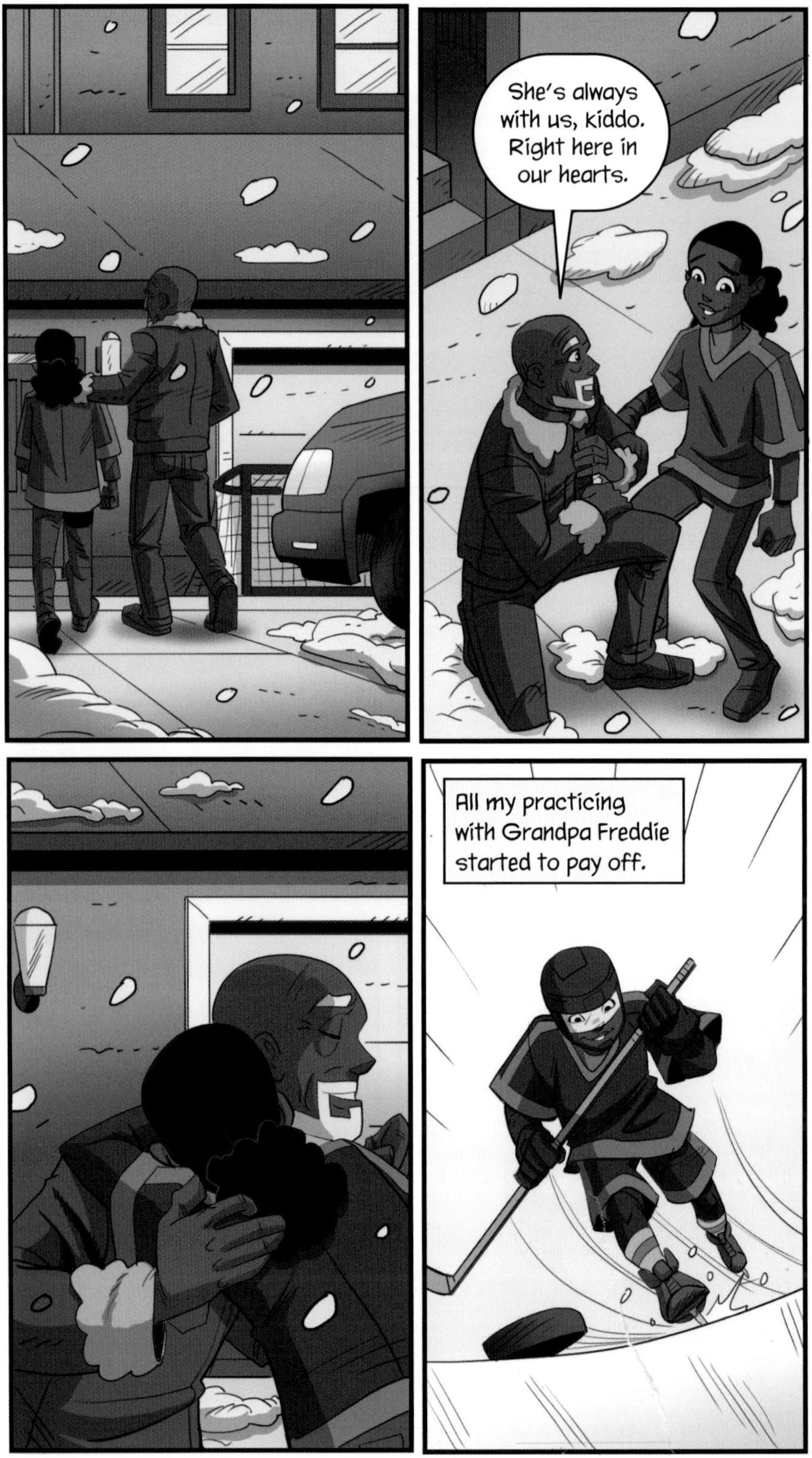
She's always with us, kiddo. Right here in our hearts.
All my practicing with Grandpa Freddie started to pay off.

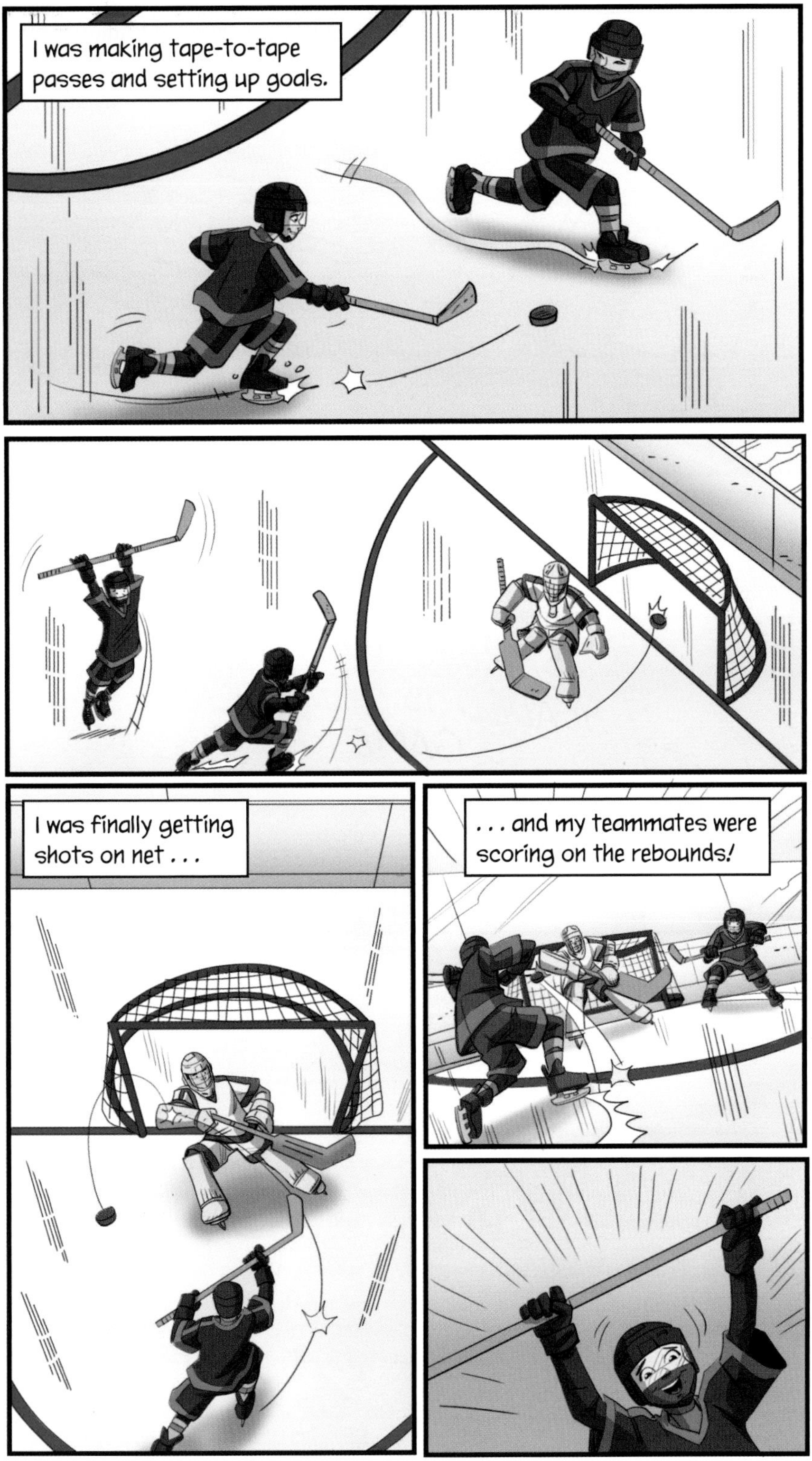
I was making tape-to-tape passes and setting up goals.
I was finally getting shots on net . . .
. . . and my teammates were scoring on the rebounds!

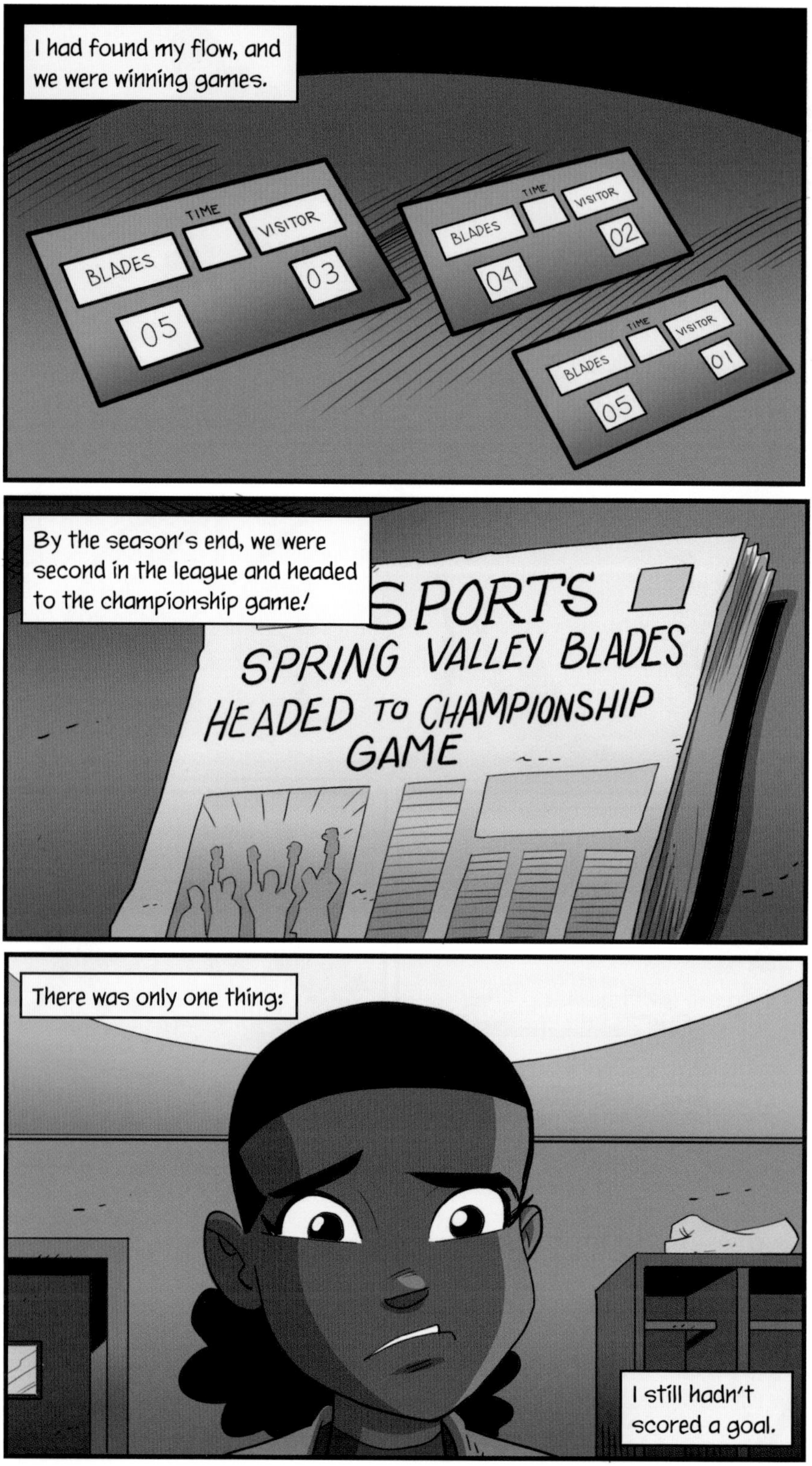
I had found my flow, and we were winning games.
BLADES
TIME
VISITOR
05
03
BLADES
TIME
VISITOR
04
02
BLADES
TIME
VISITOR
05
01
By the season's end, we were second in the league and headed to the championship game!
SPORTS
SPRING VALLEY BLADES HEADED TO CHAMPIONSHIP GAME
There was only one thing:
I still hadn't scored a goal.

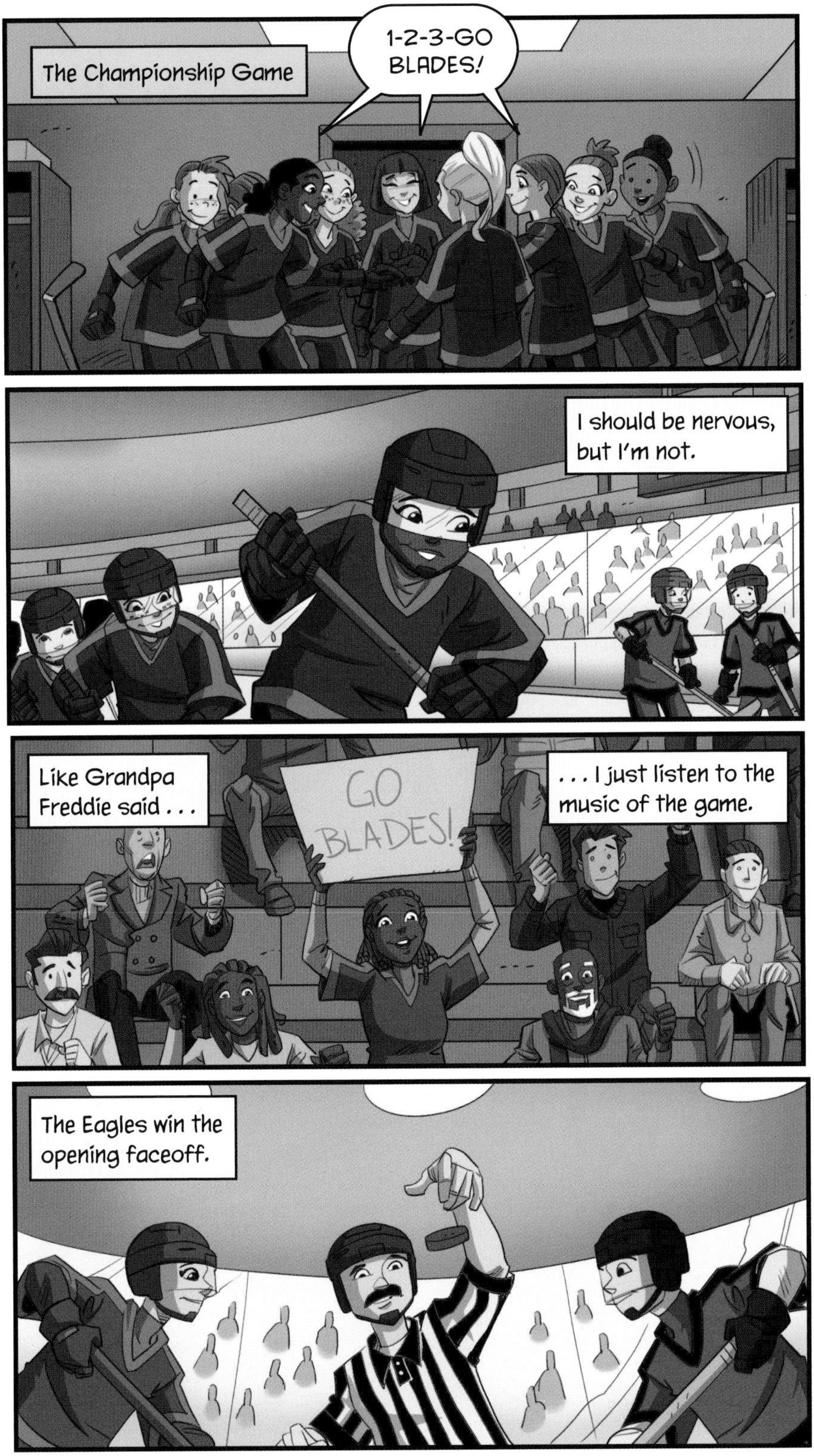
The Championship Game
1-2-3-GO BLADES!
I should be nervous, but I'm not.
Like Grandpa Freddie said . . .
GO BLADES!
. . . I just listen to the music of the game.
The Eagles win the opening faceoff.

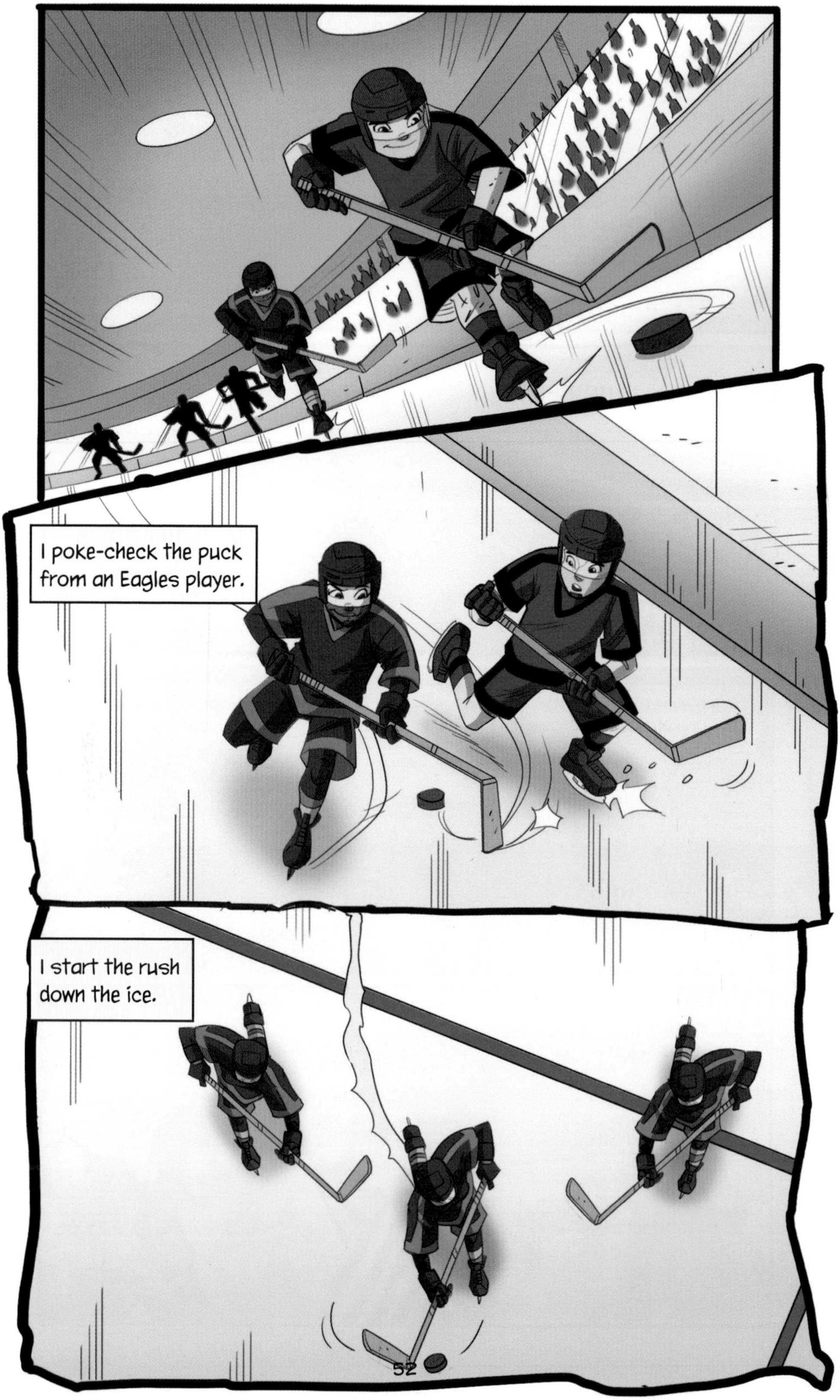
I poke-check the puck from an Eagles player.
I start the rush down the ice.

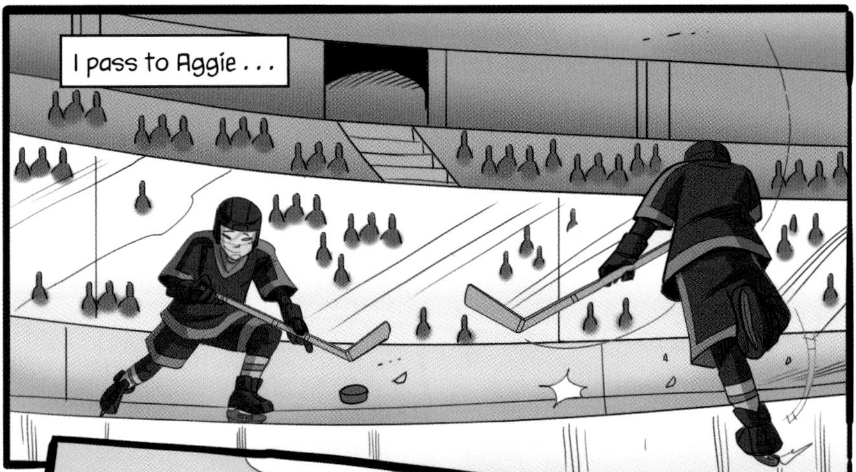
I pass to Aggie . . .

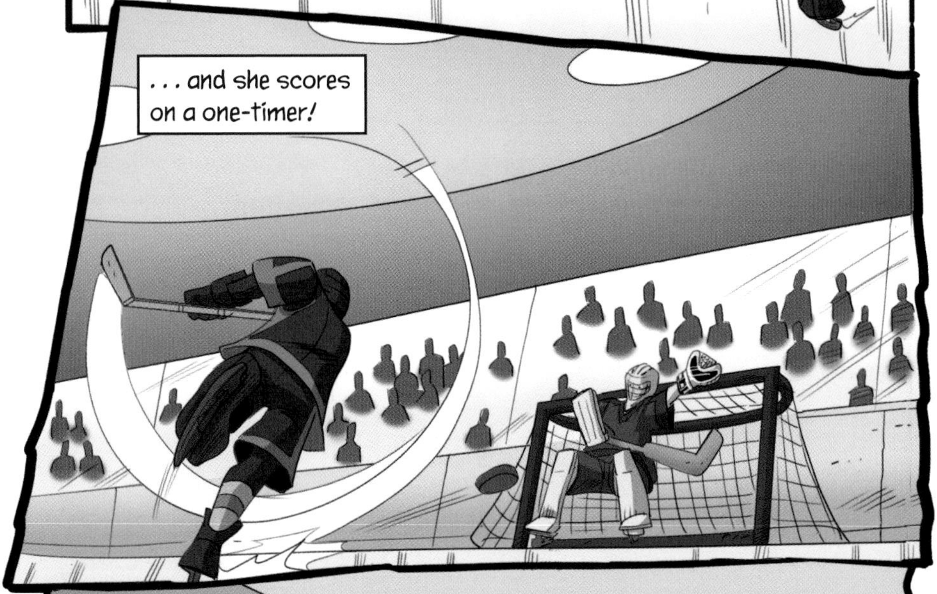
. . . and she scores on a one-timer!

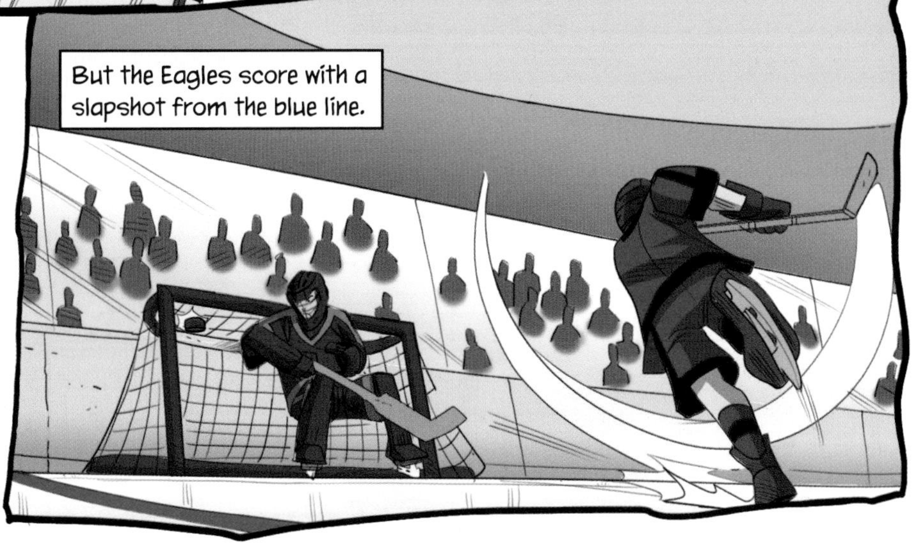
But the Eagles score with a slapshot from the blue line.

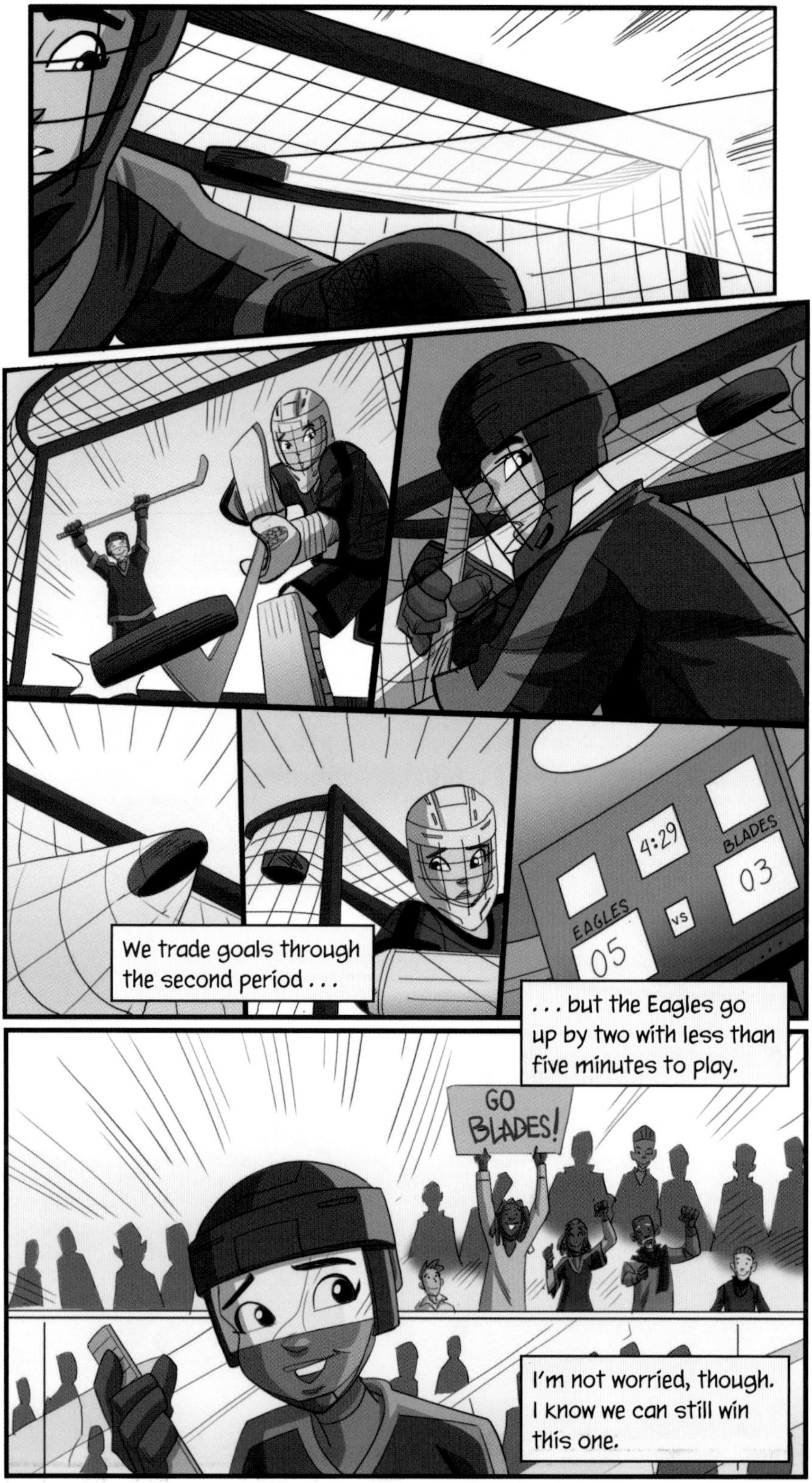
4:29
BLADES
03
EAGLES
05
VS
We trade goals through the second period . . .
. . . but the Eagles go up by two with less than five minutes to play.
GO BLADES!
I'm not worried, though. I know we can still win this one.

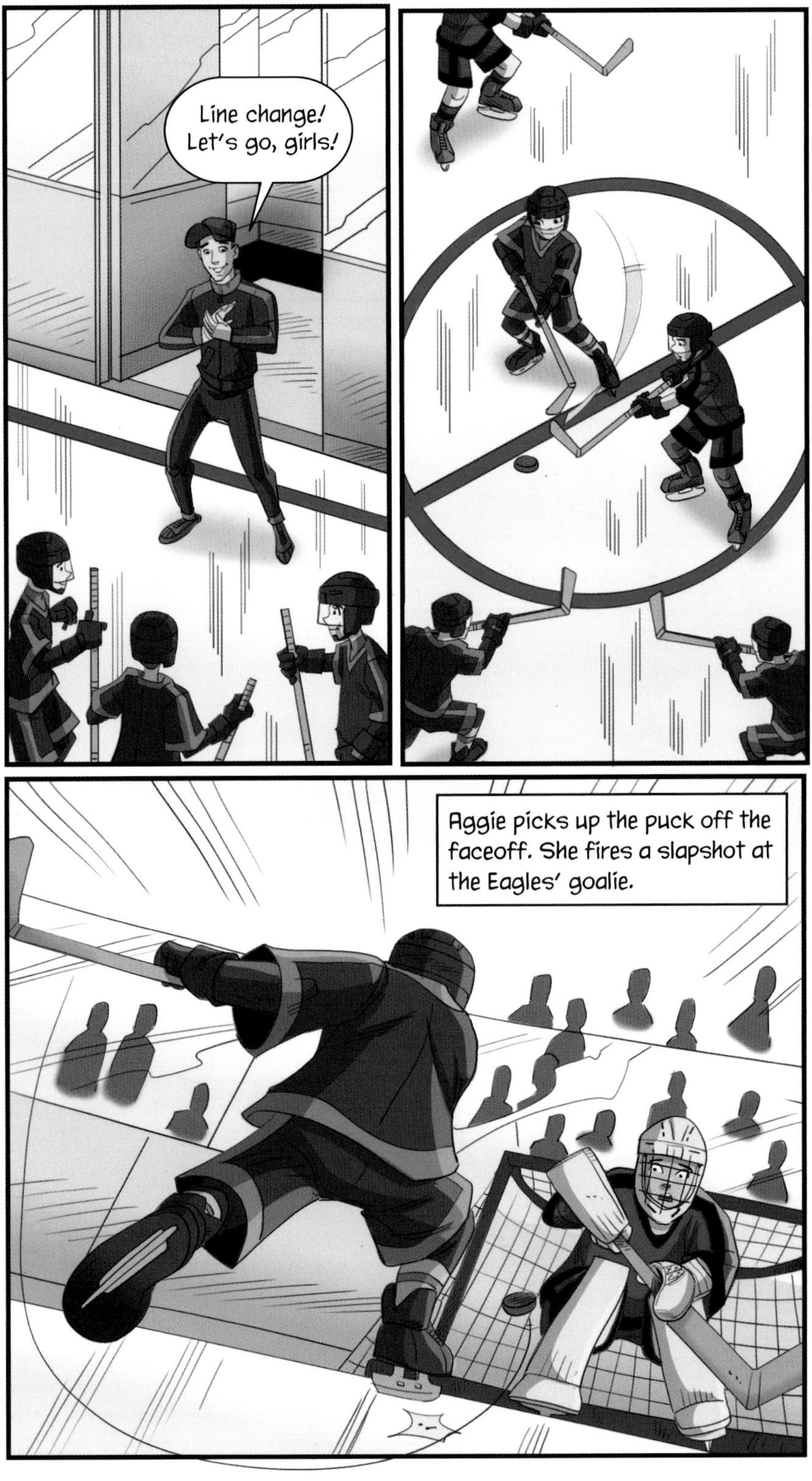

Line change! Let's go, girls!
Aggie picks up the puck off the faceoff. She fires a slapshot at the Eagles' goalie.

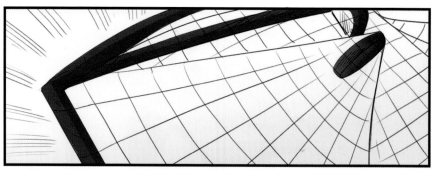

She scores to bring us within one!

Time out!

Coach Ruff calls a timeout to work out the game-tying play.

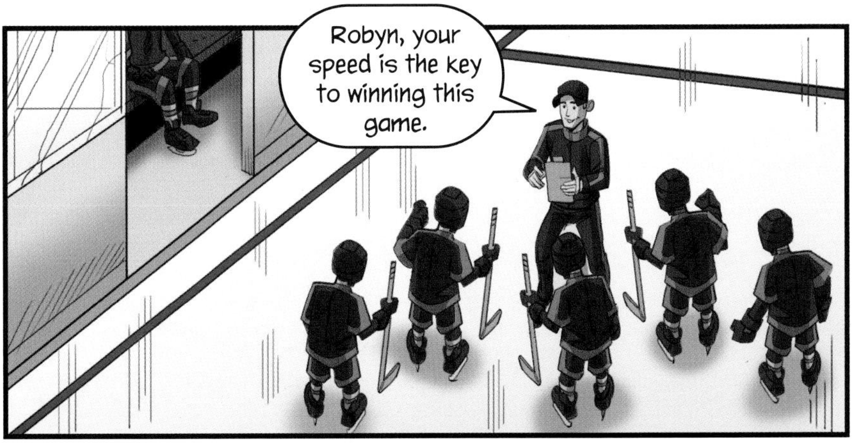
Robyn, your speed is the key to winning this game.

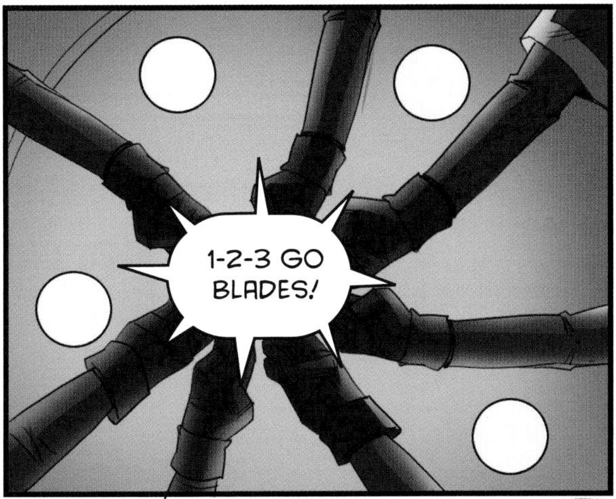
1-2-3 GO BLADES!

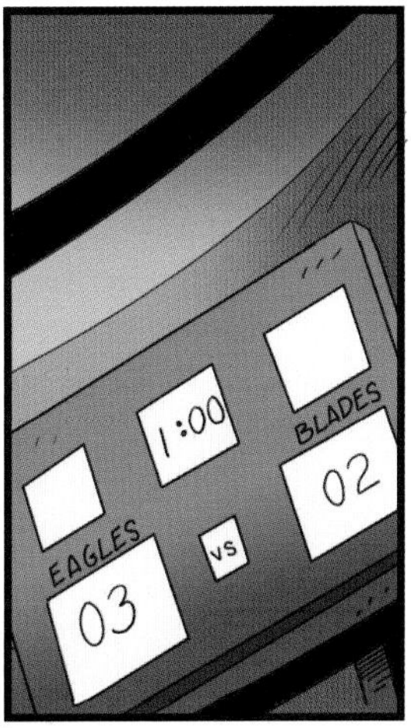
1:00
BLADES
02
EAGLES
03
VS

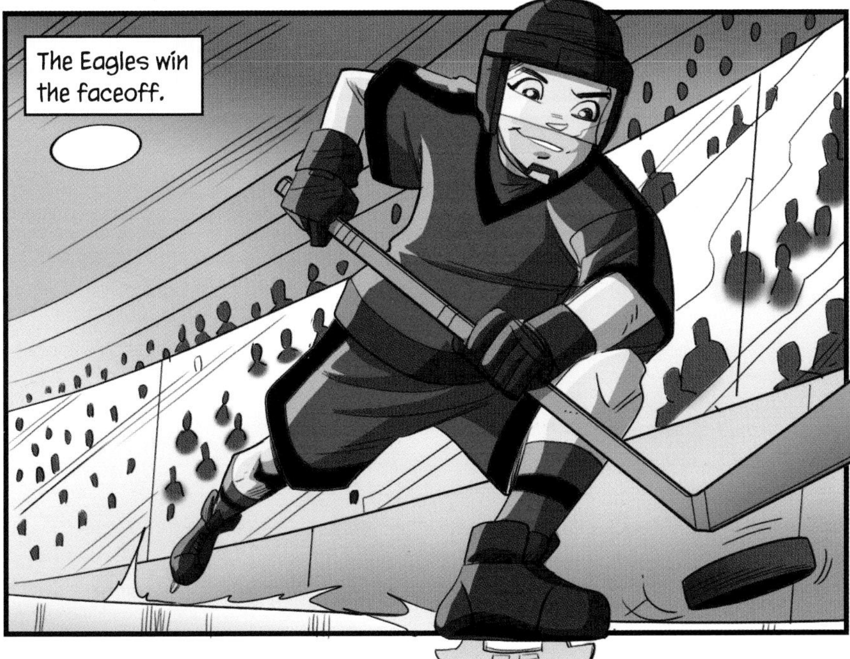
The Eagles win the faceoff.

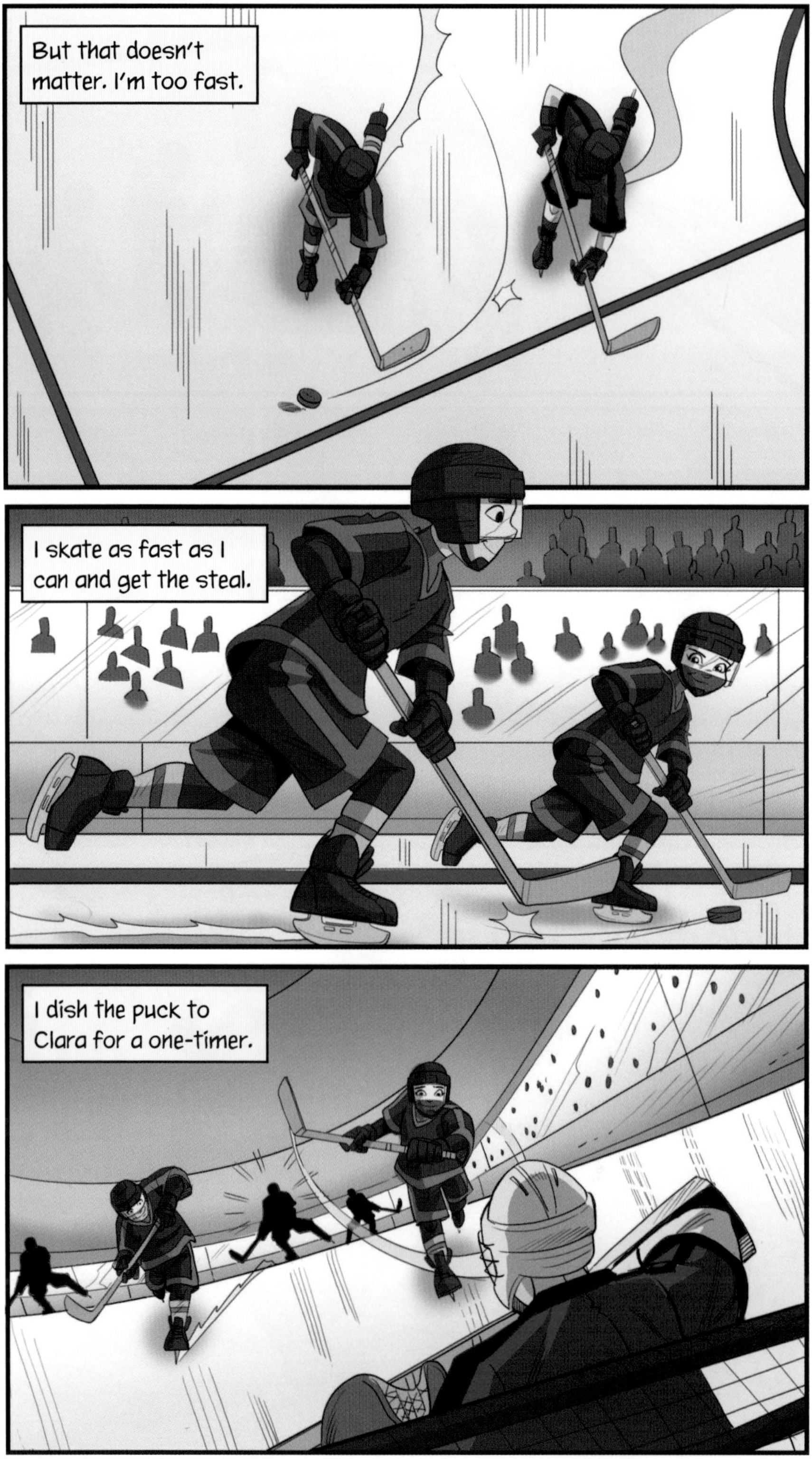

But that doesn't matter. I'm too fast.
I skate as fast as I can and get the steal.
I dish the puck to Clara for a one-timer.

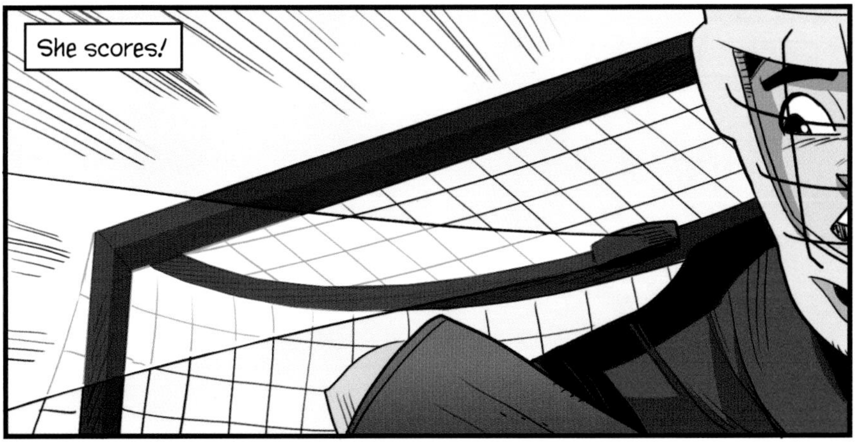
She scores!

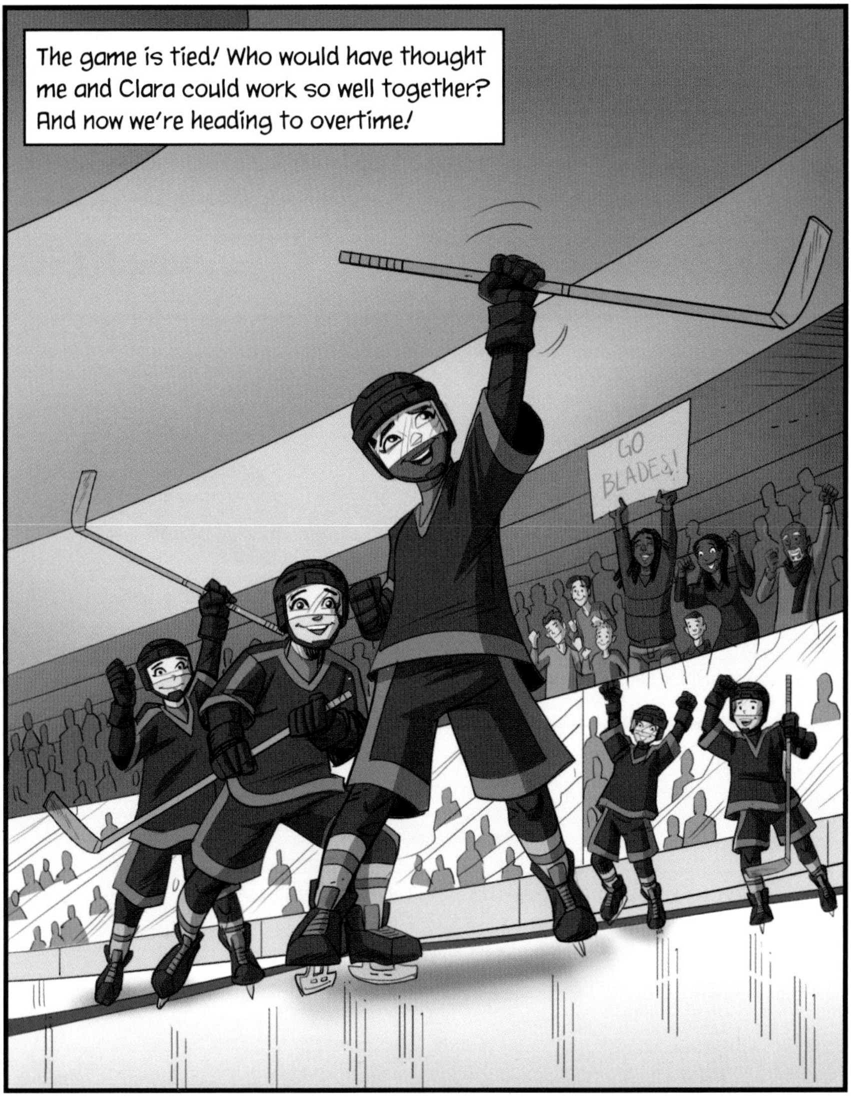
The game is tied! Who would have thought me and Clara could work so well together? And now we're heading to overtime!
GO BLADES!

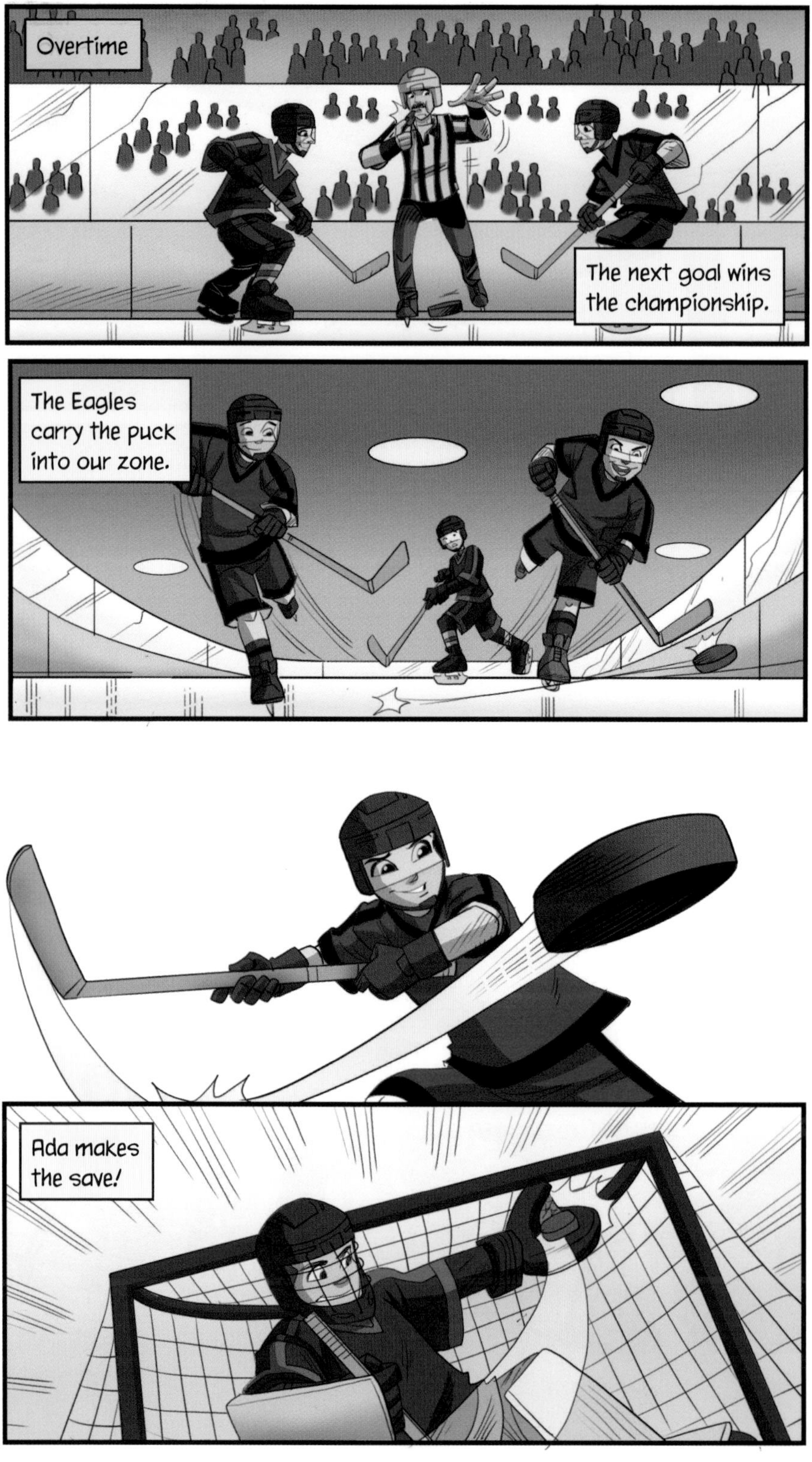
Overtime
The next goal wins the championship.
The Eagles carry the puck into our zone.
Ada makes the save!

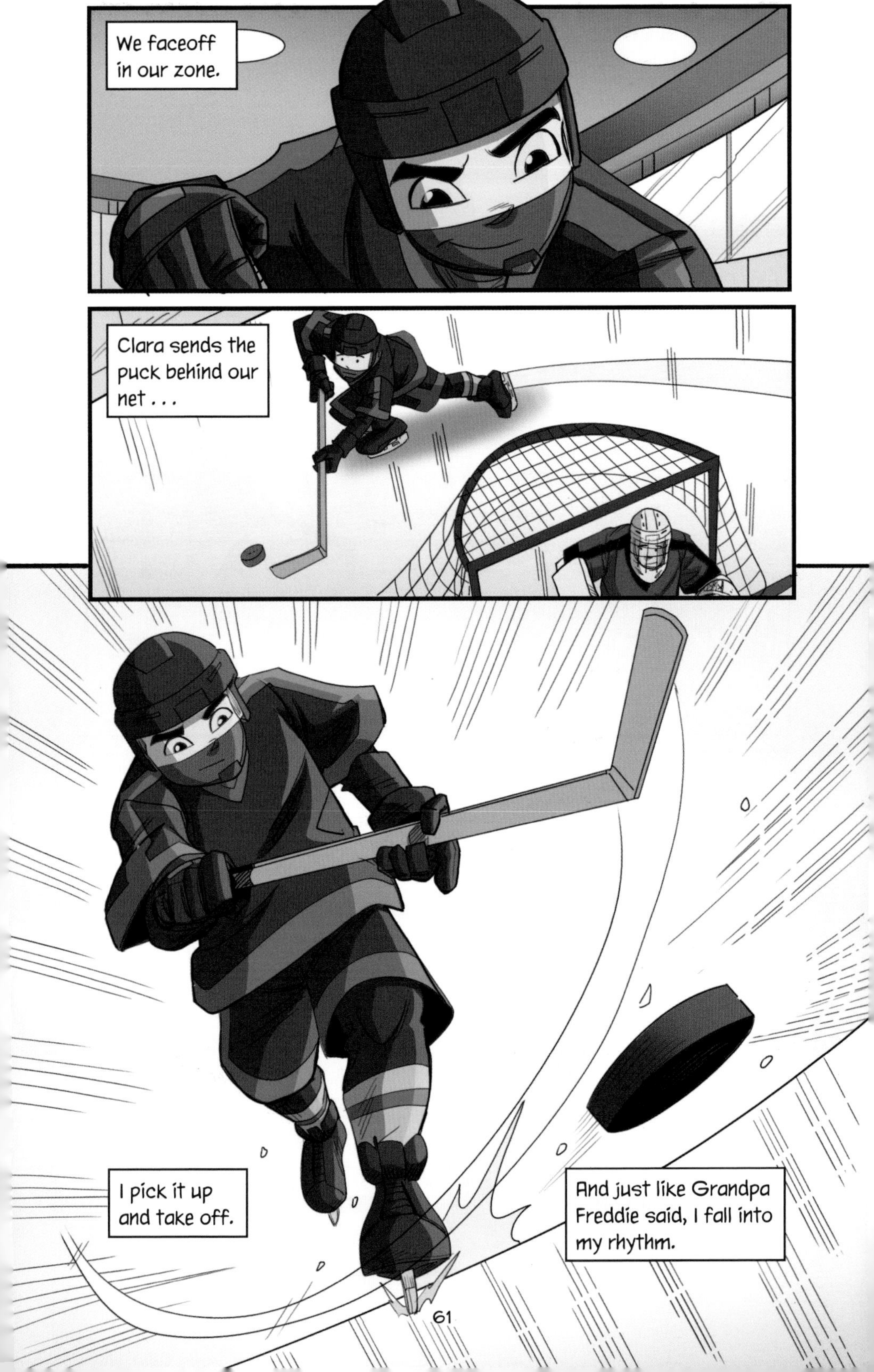
We faceoff in our zone.
Clara sends the puck behind our net . . .
I pick it up and take off.
And just like Grandpa Freddie said, I fall into my rhythm.

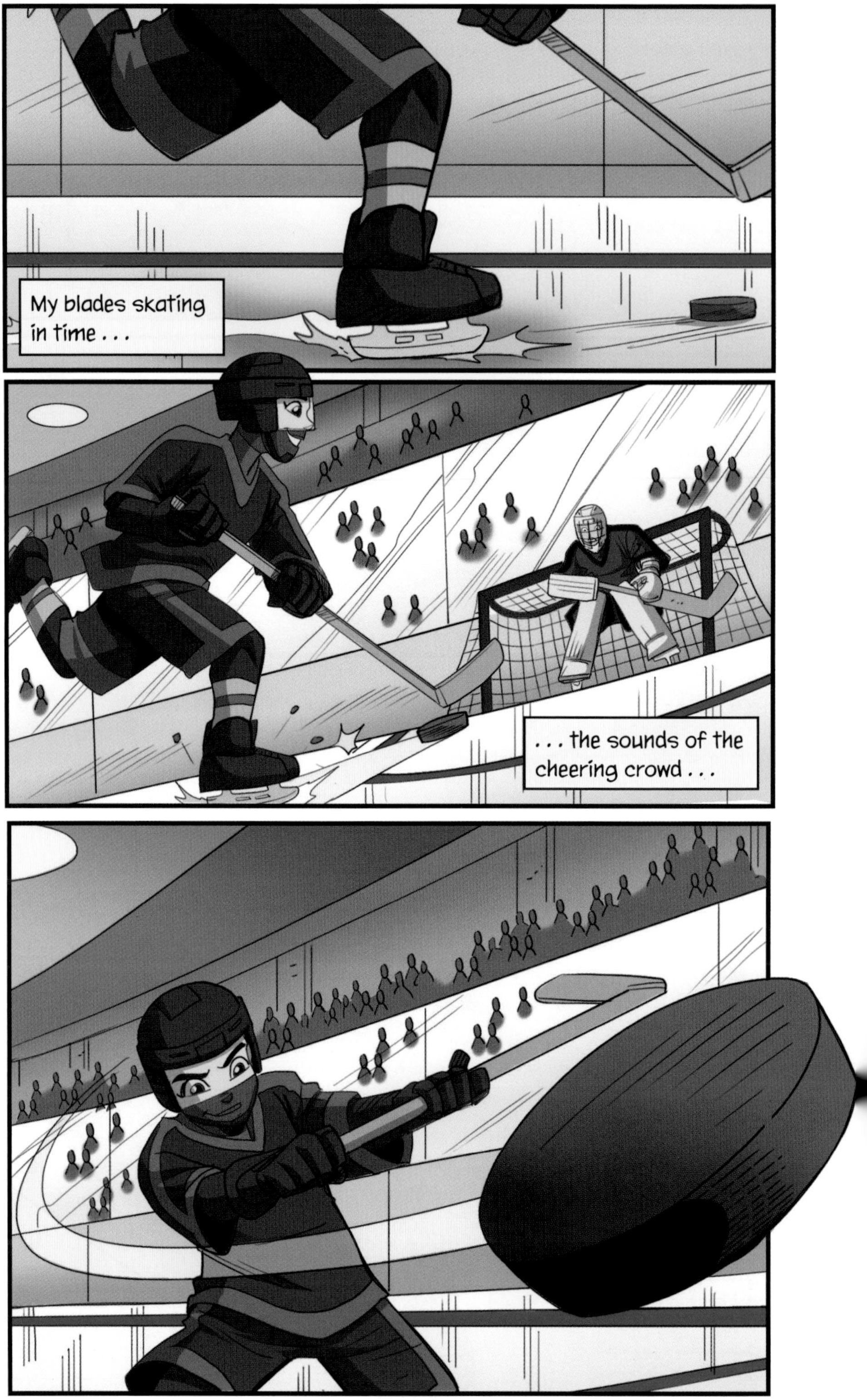
My blades skating in time . . .
. . . the sounds of the cheering crowd . . .

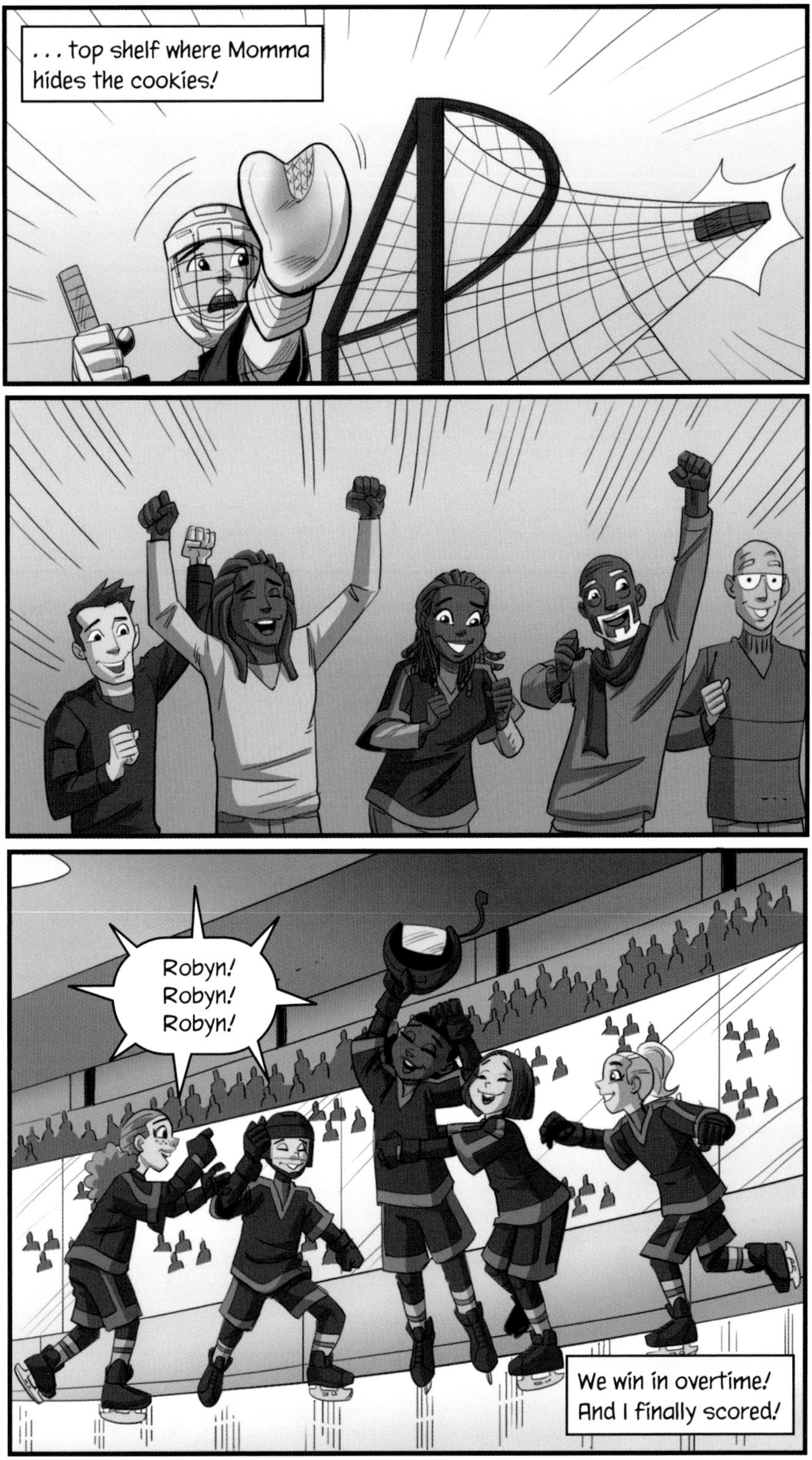
. . . top shelf where Momma hides the cookies!
Robyn! Robyn! Robyn!
We win in overtime! And I finally scored!

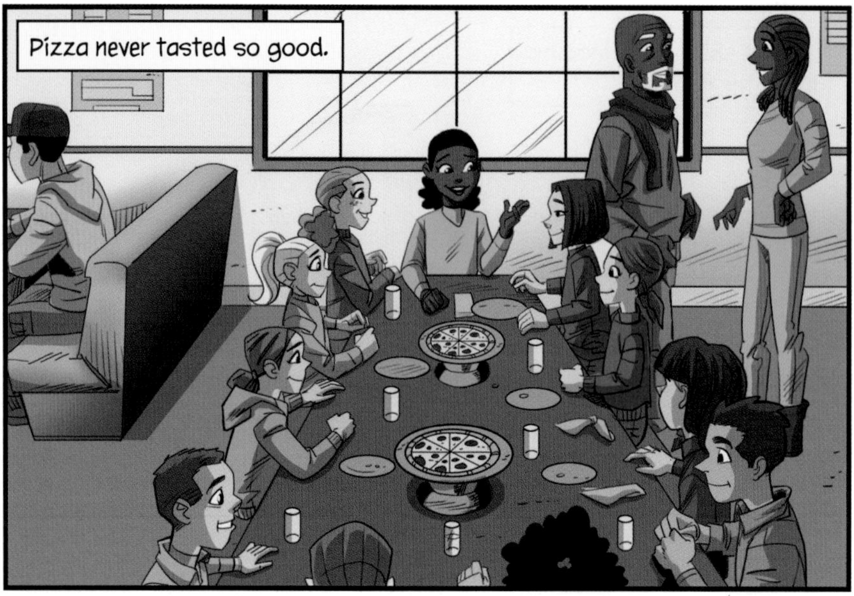
Pizza never tasted so good.

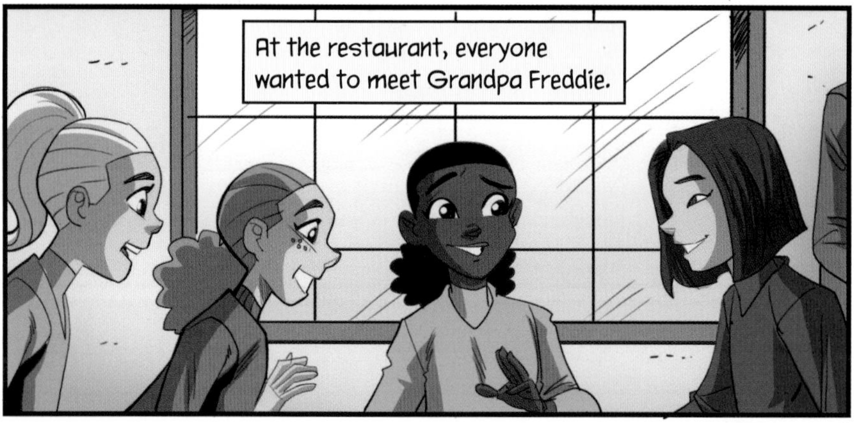
At the restaurant, everyone wanted to meet Grandpa Freddie.

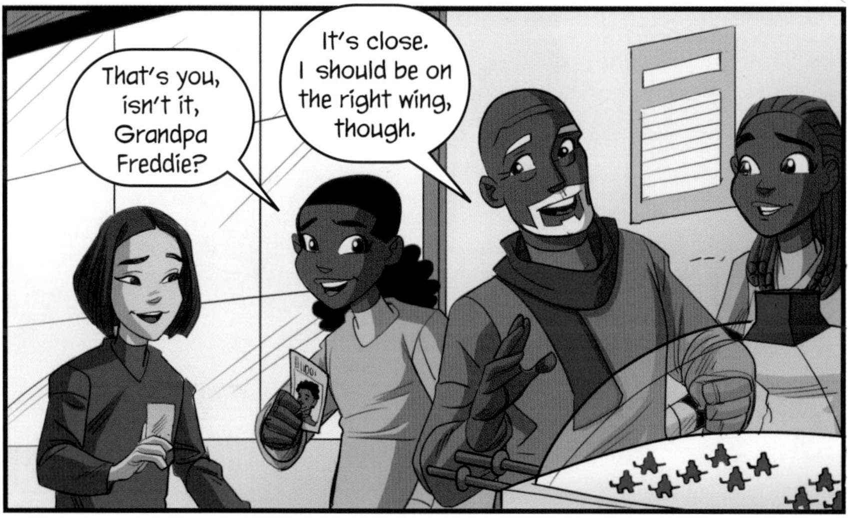
That's you, isn't it, Grandpa Freddie?
It's close. I should be on the right wing, though.

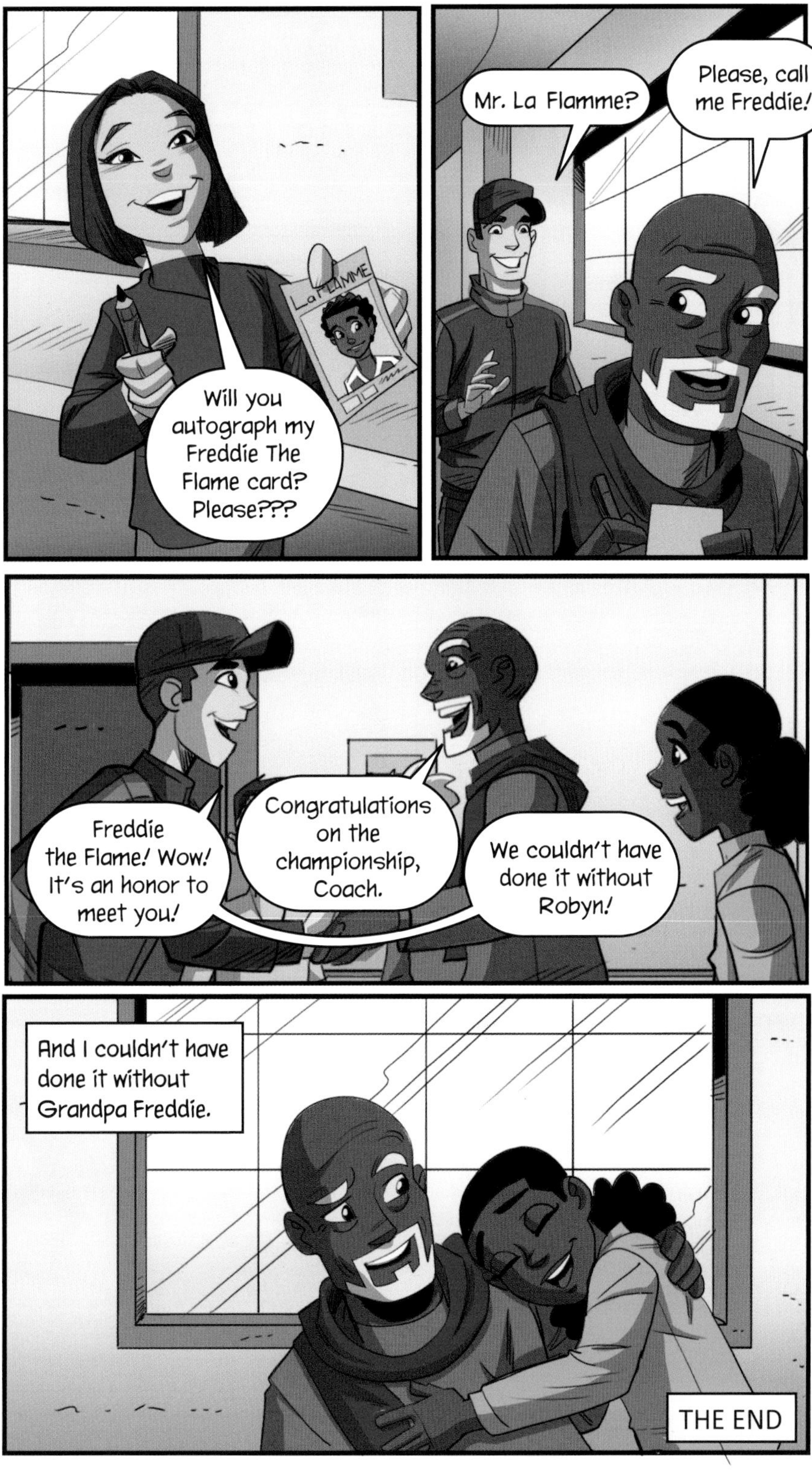
LaFLAMME
Will you autograph my Freddie The Flame card? Please???
Mr. La Flamme?
Please, call me Freddie!
Freddie the Flame! Wow! It's an honor to meet you!
Congratulations on the championship, Coach.
We couldn't have done it without Robyn!
And I couldn't have done it without Grandpa Freddie.
THE END

VISUAL DISCUSSION QUESTIONS

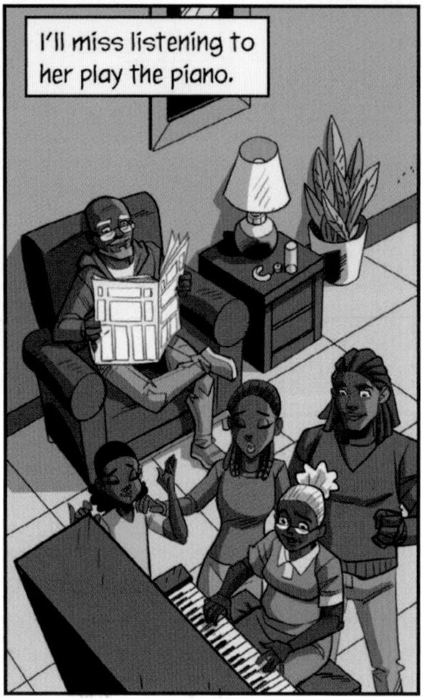

I'll miss listening to her play the piano.

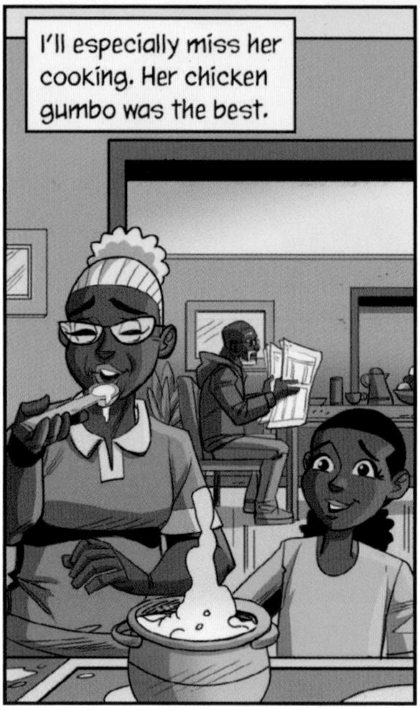

I'll especially miss her cooking. Her chicken gumbo was the best.

1. What hints does the artist give here to show that Robyn was not close with Grandpa Freddie before Grandma Evie died?

2. Art in graphic novels can show what people are thinking. What moment is Robyn thinking about here? Why do you think that is?

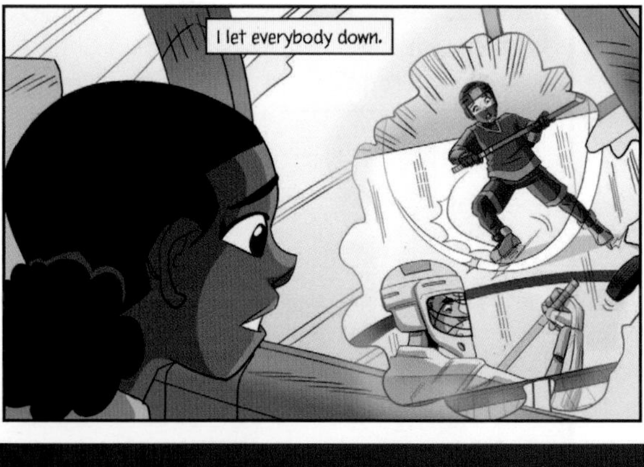

I let everybody down.

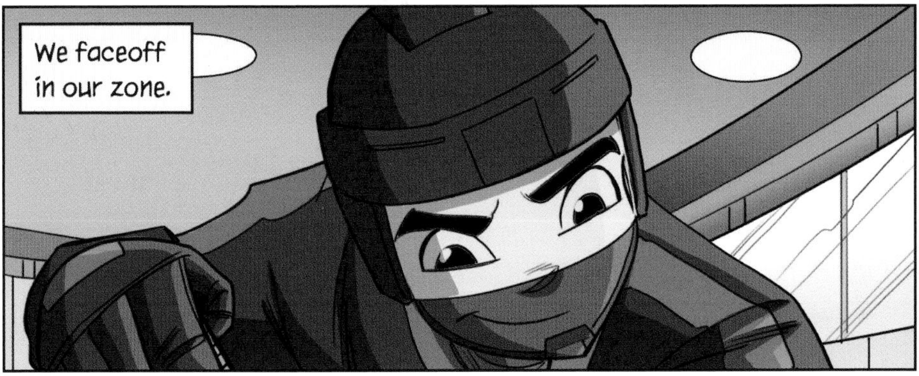
We faceoff in our zone.

3. In graphic novels, the art can often show a character's emotions better than words. What do you think Robyn is feeling in this scene? What clues make you think that?

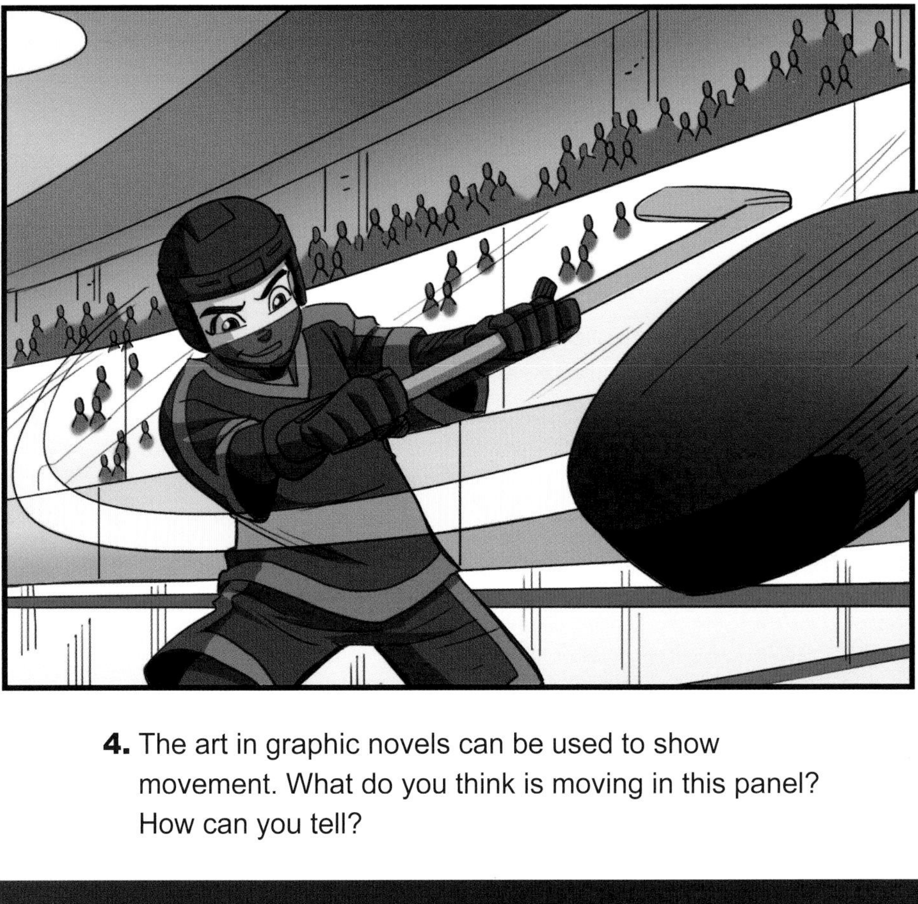

4. The art in graphic novels can be used to show movement. What do you think is moving in this panel? How can you tell?

FUN HOCKEY FACTS

On January 18, 1958, Willie O'Ree became the first Black player in the NHL. He played 45 games for the Boston Bruins and scored four goals and 10 assists. His career inspired many other players from marginalized groups, including P.K. Subban, Wayne Simmonds, and Matt Dumba. In January 2022, O'Ree received the Congressional Gold Medal for his extraordinary contributions to hockey.

If a hockey team is losing by a goal or two with a few minutes to play, they might pull their goalie. Doing this gives them an added player to help the team score. But sometimes, the other team will score on the open net.

The Zamboni was invented in 1949 by Frank Zamboni. This machine resurfaces the ice between periods to make it smooth again for the skaters.

The original Bubble Hockey game was developed with the underdog USA Olympic Hockey team of 1980 facing off against the clear favorite Russian Hockey team. That year, Team USA won the gold medal in what became known as the Miracle On Ice.

Flow is a state of mind in which a person becomes fully immersed in an activity. People who slip into a flow state often describe feelings of intense calm and focus. They even say that time seems to slow down. Flow states aren't limited to athletes and musicians—anyone can experience it when doing something they love!

HOCKEY TERMS YOU SHOULD KNOW

breakaway—when an attacking player has the puck and there is nobody between them and the goalie

coast to coast—when a single player carries the puck from their zone all the way to the opposing team's zone

deke—a move used by the puck carrier to get past a defender

enforcer—a player who tries to protect their teammates by engaging physically with opposing players

face-off—when the referee drops the puck between one player from each team; the players battle for possession of the puck to start or restart play

one-timer—when a player hits the puck without stopping it; often the most powerful and impressive shot in hockey

rebound—a puck that bounces off the goalie and remains in play

tape-to-tape—a crisp pass that goes from the tape of one player's stick to the tape of their teammate's stick

GLOSSARY

advantage (uhd-VAN-tij)—something that helps you or puts you ahead

championship (CHAM-pee-uhn-ship)—a contest to decide the best in a sport

courage (KUHR-ij)—the ability to do something that is scary

fault (FAWLT)—responsibility for an accident or misfortune

professional (pruh-FESH-uh-nuhl)—a person who makes money by doing something other people do for fun, such as playing ice hockey

regret (ree-GREHT)—to feel sad or disappointed about something, especially something that should've been done differently

Contemporary Cases in Labor–Management Relations